MW01244636

Cora's Promise

Book One of the Texas Strong Series

Sunny Marie Baker

ISBN: 0692959114
ISBN 13: 9780692959114

I lovingly dedicate this book to my father, Jack L. Lane, who believed I wrote 'a darn good story' long before I ever did. I miss you, daddy.

Special thanks to my awesome editor, Judith Heuring Hussain, and to Krista Lynn Designs for the fabulous cover art.

My undying gratitude goes to my husband, Bob, who took over all the household chores which allowed me to keep my butt in the chair and write.

Texas 1867

The Farewell

Cora knelt at the grave marker of her recently deceased husband. She kissed her fingertips and placed them against the smooth engraved wood. Her chest ached, and she couldn't catch a breath. She needed time to grieve her loss properly, but that was not a gift afforded her. "I will carry you in my heart always, dear William."

She brushed a tear from her cheek with the back of her hand. "I don't want to leave you, but there is nothing for me in Kansas now, and I gave my word. Sleep well in the arms of the angels, my love."

Cora glanced toward the marker a few feet away, placed only four days ago. She stood and walked toward it. "You were a dear friend, Berta. I'm proud to have known you. There's no need to worry. I leave in the morning to make the delivery. I will do as you asked...I will keep my promise."

Squaring her shoulders, Cora smoothed the skirt of her dress. The journey ahead would be long and at times treacherous, but there was no other choice. Her word was her bond. She closed the cemetery gate and made her way down the hill, back to the boarding house. There were last minute items to pack, and come daylight she'd start her trek to Rabbit Glen, Texas.

1

"Locke. Ramsey Locke, you about? Got somethin' to give to ya."

Ramsey glanced from the barn loft, not surprised to see Reverend Matthew Hollister. It was his habit to check on folks if they missed a Sunday at church. He'd missed several.

He shoved the pitchfork into the haymow, climbed down the ladder, and headed out the barn door.

"Reverend, guess you've come to see if I'm still among the living?"

"I have noticed your absence on the Sabbath, Ramsey." Hollister reached out a hand, and Ramsey shook it. "I know you've got a lot to make ready 'fore winter, being you're workin' your spread alone. Reckon I can understand you wantin' to catch ever bit of daylight ya can."

"Thanks, Reverend, for your tolerance. I've got a passel of work to get done, and I'm way behind point."

Ramsey gazed out over his six hundred forty-four acres of Texas dirt. "I'll get back to Sunday services soon."

"Good to hear."

"What'd you bring me, a hunk of Mary Lou's maple cake? She promised some next time she baked."

"Sorry, Locke, no cake today. Besides comin' to check on your soul, I'm deliverin' this. The minister pulled a pale yellow paper from his pocket. Jesse at the telegraph office asked if I'd mind to bring it out to ya."

"Who'd be sending me one of these?" A frown rutted Ramsey's forehead. He pulled off his work gloves, took the telegram, broke the seal and read. His eyes registered what his mind couldn't get a grip on. "Well, this is a bit of a strange." He rubbed the back of his neck and cocked his head sideways.

"Bad news?" Hollister inquired.

"Partly so."

Ramsey sucked air. It crushed against his ribs like an anvil against steel. The telegram brought a flood of memories he'd been doing his damnest to forget—a time he had no hankering to remember. "Someone I knew back in Kansas has passed. Says here she's sending me her *treasure*."

"Treasure? Like gold coins?" Hollister asked.

"That I doubt. She had a little business all right, but don't think it could've made her rich by any means." An image of the petite brunette with an ample bosom and tiny waist danced across his mind. Berta Minors had run the local brothel in Cold Springs, Kansas, but in the years he'd known her, she'd never pleasured any man, except for once.

"Was this woman a store owner?" The Reverend inquired. "Perhaps she owned stock and sold it before she passed and has willed you a nice endowment."

"Nothing like that, Reverend." Ramsey never spoke of why he'd left Kansas five years ago, and he wasn't going to spill his guts now. Some things were better left private.

The sun waned behind a cloud and the day chilled. A breeze blew lazily across the yard and embraced Ramsey like a tight-knitted shawl. He could almost hear Berta's voice. *Everything's going to be all right, Ramsey. You'll see.*

Ramsey chuckled, picked up a piece of straw that blew across the ground and twisted it around his finger. "I was lost for a long time before I got to Texas, Reverend, but one morning I woke up and decided I had to continue to live whether I wanted to or not.

"Would you like to talk about it, rid your soul of the burden, Ramsey?"

"Rather not. Talking won't change the past. Besides buying this chunk of land and working it got my head on straight. It's given me a reason to get up in the mornings. I thank the kind folks of Rabbit Glen for that."

Ramsey unfolded the telegram and reread it. "Says my delivery will arrive the day after tomorrow, coming in on the mail stage. I don't cater much to waiting around in town for it to arrive. The dang coach isn't ever on time as I recall. It seems to me that would cut into my day when I ought to be moving cattle down from the high country, Reverend." Ramsey's gut knotted tight. The last time he'd waited for a stage, his whole world shattered. He didn't care to be reminded.

"I'll be in Grover that day to pick up flour from the mill. I can retrieve your parcel in Rabbit Glen as I return, bring it to ya," Reverend Hollister offered. "You're only a few miles down the road from my place. Won't be any bother."

"I'd be obliged, but let me pay you something for your trouble," Ramsey offered.

"What I would take is a small sack of flour if you can spare it. We're all out 'til I get to the mill. Mary Lou is frettin' 'cause we won't have biscuits for supper the next two days."

"I do have flour I can spare. Come on in, and I'll spoon some into a bag." Ramsey stepped to the porch and opened the cabin door. "I've got Arbuckle's brewing. You want a cup?"

"Some coffee would sure warm my innards," Matthew Hollister answered. "Looks like we're in for an early winter. Near had frost this mornin'."

"That's a fact. The oaks down by the creek have already put on autumn colors. Reckon old Mother Nature is giving us signs to prepare for cold weather." Ramsey poured two mugs of the stout brew and sat one on the table for his guest. "Sit, take a load off."

The two men made small talk and sipped coffee together. All the while Ramsey's mind wondered—what sort of treasure was Berta Minors sending him?

Cora sat on a wooden bench outside the post office which also served as the stage stop. She was here, in Rabbit Glen. It was a smaller town than she'd imagined. Across the street a two-story clapboard building sported a sign saying: Gert's Boarding House—Fifty Cents a Night. Next door was the Bluebird Café. Perhaps she could secure a job there, once her task was finished. A mercantile and blacksmith shop composed the remainder of the town, as far as she could tell.

Out of habit, Cora smoothed the wrinkles from the royal blue taffeta dress she wore and buttoned the lighter blue jacket at the waist. Thank goodness there'd been a layover in Brenham, which afforded the opportunity for a bath. She was presentable even with three days of travel dust clinging to her clothes and hair.

A man in a clergy collar tipped his hat to her as he passed. "Good afternoon, ma'am."

Cora nodded.

The man stood at the mail clerk's window. "Jasper, I've come to fetch the parcel for Ramsey Locke. It was to be on the stage today."

"Sorry, Reverend, nothin' but mail bags delivered and a couple of passengers."

"Are you sure a package for Ramsey didn't arrive?"

"Yes sir, nothin' today. Maybe it'll come in next week."

Hearing the conversation, Cora stood. "Excuse me, but I'm seeking to connect with Mr. Locke. I've been given the responsibility to present his...."

"Well then," the Reverend interrupted. "We were expecting a parcel. This is a surprise that Ramsey's endowment would arrive by escort."

"I sent a telegram ahead of my arrival. Did Mr. Locke receive it, do you know?"

"Yes ma'am, he got it, but he's pressed to get his cattle moved down from the high country, so I volunteered to pick up his delivery. I'm Reverend Matthew Hollister." He pointed to a wagon and team standing ready in the alley. "Shall we go? I'll take you right to Ramsey's door."

Cora roused the sleeping boy sprawled on the bench. "Come, child. Our ride is here."

A two horse team clamored down the rutted road, the wagon bouncing behind. Silent thunder clouds churned overhead and gave an occasional sparse glimpse of a hazy sun. Cora curled her arms around her waist, shielding against the damp air. She'd expected Texas to be warm and sunny. *Please God, don't let this dreariness be an omen.*

"How much farther, Reverend Hollister?

She was bone weary from the long journey, and she yearned to sit on something that didn't move. Cora scanned the vast land before her. If it weren't for the scrub-scattered mountains that reached for the distant sky, it would appear much like the plains of Kansas.

"Not too far now. Over that next rise in the road." Hollister snapped the reins, and the horses followed the pitted road as it veered and yielded to a wooden bridge that crossed a flowing foliage-lined brook.

The road narrowed as it approached the top of the hill. "There's Locke's place yonder." The Reverend pointed to a modest house eighty yards or so ahead.

As they neared, a sign on the fence announced: Lost C Ranch. A log cabin sat in the center of a cleared area, a barn in need of paint to the left, and the roof-covered well on the right. A large wood plank corral lay to the north of the road where it entered the barren yard. A short walk from the house a plowed garden showed wilted green tops above the ground. Road Island Reds pecked at the ground inside the chicken coop.

Cora observed a man maneuver his horse off the ridge and down the hill toward the cabin. The clouds eclipsed the sun, and a cold wind kicked up. The air turned static and brought a chill that crawled up Cora's spine like a scorpion.

She didn't know how Ramsey Locke would accept the gift she brought, but in doing so, she'd fulfilled the promise to her dying friend, Berta. Cora shivered, hugged herself tighter. What would tomorrow bring? Where would she go from here? She had no thought. She had no plan. She had no place to be.

Ramsey arrived in front of the cabin as Reverend Hollister pulled the team to a halt. The woman in the seat beside him wasn't Mary Lou, the Reverend's wife. Mrs. Hollister was a robust woman with graying hair. The woman accompanying the Reverend was petite.

Golden ringlets of hair escaped her bonnet and framed her pale face. Most like some of Mary Lou's kin come to stay awhile. A thin, dark-haired young boy rode in the back of the wagon clutching a tattered old carpet bag. Tying his Appaloosa to the hitching rail, Ramsey dismounted. "Didn't intend to put you out any to bring my parcel, Reverend, especially now I see you got company visiting." He pulled off his gloves and shoved them into his back pocket.

"No company for me. This lovely lady has come to speak with you, Locke." Reverend Hollister tied the reins to the brake lever, disembarked to assist the young woman and the child to the ground.

For no reason Ramsey could place, panic thumped against his ribs. "Are you a courier sent to hand-deliver what Berta Minors willed to me?"

"My momma's gone to heaven and I ain't never gonna see her on this earth again," the boy shouted. He hid in the folds of the woman's skirt, his hazel-colored eyes wide and anxious.

"I'm real sorry about that, fella. I know the pain you're suffering, truly I do," Ramsey offered comfort to the boy dressed in a starched shirt, and what appeared to be new overalls. He looked to be around five or six years old. Tall for his age, the boy stood stiff, uneasy and alert, as if ready to run if the situation warranted.

The petite woman stepped forward and extended her hand. "Hello, I'm Cora Sutton. Berta hired me to care for her child during her work hours. We became friends, and it was me who tended her needs during the last months before she left us."

"Now, that's a good woman who'd help a friend in need." The Reverend said climbing into the wagon. "Git-up, now. Go." He slapped the reins. "Up to you to get the lady back to town when you're done talking," he shouted over his shoulder.

"Hang on, Hollister...you can't leave these folks here." Ramsey trotted behind the wagon a few feet, yelling protests.

Reverend Hollister slapped the reins against the horses' rumps again, waved, and never looked back.

Scratching his head, Ramsey stood one foot cocked to the side and watched the wagon disappear down the road. He turned and stomped back to where the woman and boy waited. "Miss, you want to tell me what the hell is going on?"

The woman appeared to cringe at the profanity spoken, but he wasn't in the mood to apologize. "Speak up, woman."

"I'm sorry our presence upsets you, but it was Berta's dying wish that I escort the child to you, Mr. Locke."

"This boy?" Ramsey stared at the kid, saw some unfocused memory he couldn't quite piece together. His belly flip-flopped, the fluttering wings of a yellow butterfly nearby sounded in his head like the roar of a tornado. "Why would Berta want you to do that?"

"Because, sir." Cora cleared her throat. "This is Treasure Keaton Locke. Your son."

2

amsey's knees went weak. He knew now what it was he saw in the boy—the reflection of himself. The child standing before him was a duplicate of the image in the tin-plate photo his mother kept on her dresser during his growing up years. Treasure was a chip off the frying pan, no denying that. The pain in Ramsey's temple didn't budge, even though he tried to rub it away.

"You'd better come on in. We can sit while you explain all this to me."

Once inside the woman removed the boy's jacket. "Can you sit there by the basin table, Treasure, and play with your wooden horse?" she instructed more than asked.

"Yes'um," he said and squatted on the floor in the corner of the room.

"Can I get you a cup of coffee, Miss?"

"No, but some tea would be nice if you have any."

Ramsey opened the cupboard door and pulled the tea can down, opened it and found it empty. "Sorry, I'm out."

"Then a tumbler of water would be fine."

Ramsey ladled water from the bucket on the counter, sat the glass down in front of the woman. "What did you say your name was again?"

"Cora. Cora Sutton."

He tossed some kindling into the pot-belly stove, lit it aflame, pulled out a chair and sat. "That'll take the chill off, Miss Sutton. Ramsey leaned the chair back on two legs; his feet planted firmly on the floor. "You need to start at the beginning. This boy is news to me."

"He's your offspring, Mr. Locke, sure as the sun will rise tomorrow."

Ramsey stood and went to the curtained alcove serving as his sleeping room. He returned with a small filigree framed picture and handed it to Cora. "I can see that."

"How can this be? It's Treasure." She gazed upon the picture. "Who are these other people?"

"That's not Treasure. It's me with my momma and daddy. I was five years old. I guess Treasure is about that age. There's no doubt he's my blood. I don't deny it... but...how...? As near as I can remember I only spent one night with Berta." *Of course, I was puking up, falling down drunk most of the time back then, so there could be a night or two I don't remember.*

A slight grin started to curl Cora's mouth before she pulled it into check. "Sir, if I may be so bold, it only takes one night." Cora's face heated and sweat popped beads on her forehead. "I regret I've spoken out of turn."

"You spoke the truth, Miss Sutton. Take no shame in that." Ramsey chuckled and smiled. He poured himself a cup of day old coffee he'd reheated that morning and wrinkled his nose against its cold bitterness. "You must know I didn't abandon Berta. If I'd known I'd have taken on the responsibility." Sadness crept across Ramsey's heart. He had a son, and he missed out on the first years of his life—the bonding years.

"I've not told anyone here in Rabbit Glen, but I reckon you have a right to know some things, Cora." Ramsey breathed an involuntary sigh. "I was engaged to a woman I'd met in Boston while attending medical school. Caroline came to join me in Kansas, so we could begin to plan our wedding." Ramsey took a long swig of the bitter coffee, grit his teeth and swallowed.

"I saw the stage arriving, a bit early, so I wasn't at the stage stop but a few feet away. A bunch of rowdies had come into town early that morning and were in the saloon across the street from where the stage parked. Caroline saw me when she disembarked. Her smile lit up the day. I rushed toward her, and she did to me. She'd taken only a couple steps when the cowpokes came out of the saloon shooting off their guns. My sweet Caroline was hit in the crossfire. Ramsey squeezed his eyes against the memory. *I'm so sorry, Caroline. I failed you. Forgive me.*

"Oh, Mister Locke, I am so saddened by the turn of events. Berta mentioned you'd had a troubling period before you left Kansas."

"I stayed drunk that first year after Caroline died in my arms. I was a trained physician, and I couldn't save her. I pressed my hand against the wound in her stomach, but the blood continued to flow, staining her beautiful green satin dress. She took one last breath and was gone." Ramsey looked away toward the window. "I couldn't even muster the fortitude to return to Boston and attend her burial. When I slept, I was plagued with horrible nightmares, saw my hands dripping with her blood. The whiskey was the only thing that gave me respite, so I drank a lot of it."

He remembered. It was on one of those, oh so many, cold rainy drunken nights when Berta put him into a warm bed and pulled the blankets around him that he'd taken her in his arms and kissed her passionately. She'd resisted. *Please, Berta, he pleaded. I want to feel a woman in my arms again, need to forget my sorrow if only for a moment.*

She allowed him to make love to her that night, had responded in kind. He awoke the next morning, spent and hung over, and knew this wasn't the life Caroline would want him to live—wallowing in liquor, giving affection to a woman for which he had no love. She'd insist he wash his face, comb his hair, pull on his boots and move forward to bring about the dream they'd envisioned. Her face, smiling and gentle appeared on the wall of the cabin. It floated across the window like a foggy mist. Ramsey shook the image from his mind, blinked to be sure it was gone.

"Mister Locke, are you well? You've turned pale.

"Yes, I'm right up. Remembering is a strain sometimes. It seems a long time ago, yet like it was this morning."

"It's been some years now, are you still plagued with bad dreams?"

"Once I got to Rabbit Glen I found my footing. I'd been able to keep my sadness at bay, was doing fine until...now."

"So my arrival with Treasure has brought this horrendous event back to your doorstep." Cora shook her head. "I'm sorry, Mister Locke, I had no idea. My objective was to do Berta's bidding. She so wanted Treasure to grow up with one of his parents and not pawned out to some family who'd use him as a work hand. She wanted him to know love with someone he could love in return."

Cora raised her hand toward him but quickly replaced it in her lap. "You understand?"

"I do, but I'm trying to figure why Berta never told me about the child." Ramsey sat, crossed his ankle over one knee and bounced his foot. "It was near a month after...our encounter before I left Cold Springs."

Cora removed her traveling gloves and laid them neatly on the rough-hewn sawbuck table. "By the time she realized she was expecting you'd departed. She asked around, but it seemed no one knew where you'd gone. Treasure was over a year old when the town blacksmith mentioned you'd bought his cousin's ranch. However, he wasn't even sure where in Texas it was located. So, Berta figured it was best to raise the boy on her own and not bother you. She had no idea she wouldn't live to accomplish that task."

Ramsey sat silent a moment, head bowed. The pain in his brain pounded like the tom-toms of a war party. "How'd she die?"

"Doc Brewer said consumption. I think the medical men say that when there's no name to put on what ails a person. No offense intended, Mr. Locke, toward your medical expertise."

"None taken, Miss Sutton."

Berta got real sick, and for the last six months, I was her caretaker, watched over her needs and took responsibility for Treasure."

Cora unbuttoned her lightweight Eton jacket. "May I remove my outer garment? Your wood stove makes the room toasty warm."

"Of course, be comfortable. Can I get you more water?"

"No, thank you. I'm sated." Cora cleared her throat. "Berta made me promise I'd find where you'd settled and bring the child to you. She insisted he not be pawned off to strangers. I vowed I'd see he got to you. I've kept my promise."

Ramsey stared out the window to the hills beyond. A cloud haloed the yellow-orange sun setting behind a purple horizon. Darkness would creep in soon and steal the day. He had to figure out what to do with the woman and child left on his doorstep. He was in way over his head, and it didn't take a blind man running to see it. *Time—I need time to think this through.*

"Miss Sutton, I know nothing of raising a kid." He leaned in, lowered his voice and made a plea. "I've already missed out on some important years in this boy's life. I'd have to learn everything from scratch." Ramsey locked eyes with Cora's blue ones. "Couldn't you take him back to Kansas, keep him with your family? You said you'd been caring for him. I would send you money each month for his needs and come to visit as often I could."

An exasperated sigh escaped Cora's lips, and Ramsey noticed her shoulders drop. Her proper posture slumped to that of an unwanted pup.

She raised her lashes, gazed at him and sighed again. "I'd be more than happy to raise Treasure, Mr. Locke, I love that little boy, but truth told I have no family. When I leave here, I don't know where I'll end up. I have no home to which I can return."

"You don't have someone back in Kansas? I'm a bit confused."

Cora locked her fingers together, white-knuckled in her lap, and gazed at the floor. "I grew up on the east coast. My father owns a large company, Billings Shipping and Export. Unfortunately, he's disowned me," Cora stated and returned her gaze to Ramsey.

He could see the hurt in her eyes and his heart constricted. "Why would a father do that?"

The fragile woman appeared as if she might fracture into pieces. Ramsey's shoulders burred. *If you fall apart, I guarantee I'll put you back together.* Ramsey laid his hand against hers and patted protectively.

"One day while I visited my father at his office, I observed one of the dock workers looked upon me with... interest."

A blush tinted her pale cheeks. "I can see why that might be the case." Ramsey smiled. "Go on, please."

"William was oh, so handsome, with the most beautiful amber eyes I'd ever seen. His smile assured me he was a gentleman of integrity and sincerity." Cora twisted in her chair. "We began to meet in secret, fell in love and married without my father's approval. He believed I'd married beneath my stature."

"And what did you think?" Ramsey asked.

"It didn't matter to me that William warranted no position in society, or he had little money. I loved him for the gentle soul he was."

"Your father never came around I take it?"

"My father is an unforgiving man. William was fired from his job on the dock, and Father made it impossible for him to find employment in the area. We decided to come to Kansas. He knew he could find work with the railroad. They were building a link to the Transcontinental Railway. We planned to save some money and venture on to California once the link was completed. We hoped to find a nice little section of land and build a life together."

Cora smoothed her skirt with trembling hands. "Mr. Locke, I've burdened you with my troubles. I fear I've told you far more than you have any desire to know. Forgive me."

"No need. I'm interested." Ramsey got caught up in the way her mouth moved when she talked; pink and vulnerable. Ramsey scratched his head. "I don't see your complication, though. If you and your husband came to Kansas together and he found work, why do you not have someone to return to?"

Tears pooled Cora's eyes, and Ramsey noticed her throat tighten when she swallowed hard.

"My husband died only two months ago. Dynamite explosion. They were blasting through rock to lay rail, and somehow the fuse was cut too short. He couldn't outrun the destruction. I buried him in the cemetery on the hill. A few weeks later, I buried Berta in that same cemetery. As soon as her grave marker was placed, I set out to keep the promise I'd made to my friend." Cora gazed at Ramsey. "Like you, Mr. Locke, I left my sadness in Kansas."

"I'm sorry for your loss, ma'am. I know the pain of losing someone you love.

I wish I could tell you it gets better but I'd be lying. What I can tell you is this, you'll get to a point where you can make it through a day, a week, a month without thinking about them every minute. You'll find within yourself the strength to keep going."

"That is a comfort. Thank you."

"Miss Sutton, I don't mean to sound cold, but there's no way I can take on a young'un the age of this child. I'm out on the range for days at a time, sleeping on the ground, fighting rattlers. I couldn't take a small boy with me, and he's too young to leave at the cabin alone."

"I may have a solution, Mr. Locke." Cora squared her shoulders. "I'm planning to inquire at the Bluebird Café once you return me to town. I'm hoping I can secure a position there, perhaps helping to cook or serve customers. If that was the case, you could bring Treasure to me before you leave out to do range work." Cora sensed Ramsey wanted to interrupt, but she didn't give him space. "Treasure could stay in my care until you returned to fetch him. You would have to pay for his board at the boarding house, as my funds are running low. I do not know the amount of wages I might earn, so I'm unsure if my income could support myself and the child."

"That'd put a bit of a strain on me, Miss Sutton. It's an hour's ride into town to deliver Treasure to your care, and then another hour back before I could even start my day's work. That might work in the spring and summer months, not sure about the rest of the seasons."

Ramsey stood. "I'll take you and the boy back into town this evening, put you up at Gert's. I need some time to think about all this. Figure how this situation could be best handled." Ramsey tittered like a man on a tightrope. Cora had stepped up and offered to continue to care for Treasure. He, on the other hand, had balked at extending his workday by two hours. *What the hell is wrong with you, Ramsey? You're sacred poopless, that's the problem.*

He sat back in the chair, arms on his legs; he twirled his thumbs. He tackled poisonous snakes and bobcats, surely he could manage a small child. He'd need a little help, that was a given. "Miss Sutton, I believe you have a sound solution if in fact, you can secure employment at the Café. However with winter approaching that might not be an option open to you. I need some time to get my head around all this and figure out how to make it work." Ramsey rubbed his hands through his hair. "Meantime, I'll pay for you and the boy to stay at the boarding house."

"Yes, of course." Cora fidgeted, pulled a handkerchief from her beaded handbag. "I'm going to be brazenly bold, Mr. Locke, but hear me out. If you could see your way clear to allow me to stay on here, at the cabin, I'd care for Treasure while you're away with your ranch duties. I'd cook, clean and keep the clothes washed. All I would require of you in return is my room and board. I would happily sleep in the barn when you are on the premises, as I see you have only one sleeping room. Please give my idea consideration before you answer. It could present a simple fix for both of us."

Ramsey glanced to the corner where Treasure lay sprawled on the floor, toy horse clutched in his hand. His eyes fluttered, fighting sleep. "Treasure is my son, no way around that, and I don't deny it. I reckon I should be as much of a father to him as I can, now that I have the opportunity. On the other hand, I've got to make this spread pay for itself, and that means long days in the saddle."

He propped his elbows on the table. "I wouldn't be home most nights anyhow until the snow blankets in drifts. I'd be an easier task for me to bunk in the barn. There's a tack room in the back, and it's got a small wood stove. It'll be a warm shelter. You'll sleep in the cabin with the boy...if you're sure you're willing to stay."

Cora's smile lifted her cheeks and crinkled her eyes. "Oh yes, Mr. Locke, I most certainly am. I'll take excellent care of Treasure and your lodgings. Are you sure the arrangement is to your satisfaction?"

"Appears to be, ma'am. I'll get word to Reverend Hollister, let him know our plan and sleeping arrangements. Don't want him thinking we're keeping one another company. That we're living in sin."

"Yes, of course. That is a priority."

The first drops of the impending storm tapped against the kitchen window. Ramsey would be riding in the sludge tomorrow if he could get out of the barn at all. He stood, walked toward the sleeping room. "I'll clear a drawer in the chiffonier, and you can unpack your things."

He moved his shirts and long johns to a shelf above the wood bin. He'd conceded to a fair arrangement for all concerned. Of course, he wasn't sure how he'd feel after a night sleeping on a straw bed in the barn, caressed by the odor of fresh horse dung. In the morning he might decide to change his mind.

Cora made a pallet on the floor of the main room then moved a sleeping Treasure onto it and covered him with a blanket. She poured the last hot water from the kettle into a basin and carried it to the sleeping room. Undressed, she bathed the best she could and donned a clean gown. So, this was her lot. She'd live in a Texas town she knew nothing about, with a man she'd only met, caring for his son and his house. This wasn't the life she planned, not the life she dreamed, but here she was all the same.

Droplets of rain slid down the window pane. Cora traced them with her finger to where they pooled against the wood frame and disappeared. It was a moonless night, dark and dreary. She hoped the sun would shine tomorrow—she could use a bright day.

She pulled down the covers and climbed into bed. It was softer than she'd imagined, warm and embracing. Her time of grieving was over. William and Berta were gone. She and Treasure were alive, and it was time to concentrate on making a new life. The arrangement made between her and Ramsey Locke was functional, she couldn't argue the fact. It filled a need for both of them. She had a roof over her head, food to partake, and woman's work to do with a child she loved underfoot. It was an honorable life. Could one hope for more?

3

utumn leaves began to wither and brown. The wind snapped them from the tree branches, and they spiraled onto the dormant ground. Since Cora landed at Ramsey's doorstep, they'd settled into a comfortable routine. She was easy to have around. Now that the days were shorter and the temperature dropping he spent most evenings at the cabin. He'd come to enjoy the contentment he got sitting across the table from Cora—like this morning.

She absentmindedly traced the rim of her coffee cup with her delicate fingertip while Treasure babbled on about what the two of them could accomplish that day. Cora smiled and nodded, tousled Treasure's hair and laughed at his goings-on. The sound of her happiness healed Ramsey's soul like a balm. How lucky William had been to share a part of his life with her. He reckoned he might like some of that luck.

"I'll be sticking close to home today," Ramsey said. "Got some repair work to do in the barn before winter slams us."

"In that case, after I tend to the hens, I'll start the makings of a berry cobbler. We can enjoy a piece at supper," Cora said.

"If'n you're gonna be rollin' out pie dough, think you might make a circle of it baked with sugar and cinnamon for me to taste?" Treasure placed his hands in prayer position. "Please."

"I might conjure up such a treat if you're up to scooping out the chicken coop. Are you?"

"It ain't my favorite chore, but for a pleasure like sugared pie crust, I reckon I can gumption up." Treasure licked his lips and rubbed his hands together.

"You'd better finish up your breakfast, son. You're burning daylight, and so am I." Ramsey got up from the table. "Mighty fine grub, Miss Sutton. Thank you."

"Glad it agreed with you, Mr. Locke. I'll ring the dinner bell when I have the evening meal prepared." Cora picked up the empty plates from the table. "If you get hungry beforehand the left-over biscuits and salt pork will be on the counter, covered with a tea towel.

Ramsey nodded and left the house. He needed to busy himself, get his mind turned in another direction, because thinking about Cora as he was, made it difficult to get the chores finished. He found himself anxious to get back to the cabin and sit in her company. She'd turned a house into a home, and it made his heart happy.

The sun rose high in the sky. Autumn blessed them with an Indian Summer day, which was typical of Texas, before the onslaught of winter. Ramsey leaned his shoulder lazily against the barn and watched. Cora gathered eggs from the nest. The sunlight reflected off her golden hair, making a halo around her head. Damp ringlets clung to her sun-scorched neck. What he wouldn't give to kiss that beautiful neck and sooth the soreness away. Her slight frame and rounded bosom caused his body to react in a way he couldn't control. He was a man, after all, and he'd been a long time alone. On more than one night the image of her soft curves crept into his dreams and woke him, hard and wanting. He hadn't acted on his desire because what he held for Cora was more than physical attraction. He was pretty sure she'd captured his heart, and he sure as hell hadn't put up a fight.

Cora unbuttoned the top of her dress and fanned the fabric to and fro to cool. She'd discarded the crinoline petticoats she normally wore, and her firm, round bottom was defined by the skirt hanging over her body. His groin tightened against the restriction of his breeches, and he imagined his hands roaming over her naked skin. In a most uncomfortable way, like today, Cora validated that he wanted this woman in his life, and his bed. The problem was the woman he craved gave no indication she longed for him. Her behavior was nothing but appropriate. Not a single sideways glance or off-handed touch that might offer him any encouragement. Offer any reflection that she yearned for him. Offer any hope.

He turned away from the image that tortured him, pressed his hand against the hardness and tried to push it away. A useless effort. Against his better judgment, he took one last glance and observed Cora bending to retrieve eggs from the hens' nests. He could see her cotton bloomers beneath the long skirt. "Ohhhh," he groaned.

At that moment, he wanted nothing more than to act on his primal instincts; race to her, rip the material away that separated her soft, warm flesh from his need and take her right there, pressed against the wire of the chicken coop. He imagined her legs wrapped around him, opening to take him into her warmth. Of course, he wouldn't act on his impulse. He respected Cora and the boundaries she set. He wasn't about to climb the tree until she nailed steps to the trunk.

"Dammit to hell." Ramsey bent over to relieve the pressure in his loins.

"What's the matter Papa, your breakfast gravy sour in your belly?" Treasure propped himself on the top rail of a stall. "I thought it was smack-lickin' good."

Grateful for the diversion that would allow his discomfort to return to a normal state, Ramsey looked over his shoulder at the boy he'd come to care about more than he'd thought possible. "Didn't see you run in here,."

"I crawled through the hole over there." Treasure pointed to the back wall of the barn where a board had partially broken away.

"You turning raccoon on me, boy?"

The child giggled, climbed down and joined his father. "Better get me some nails and a hammer and get that hole fixed, I reckon."

"Yep, I reckon." Ramsey ruffled his son's ebony hair. Treasure would turn six in another few months, and he was smart like a fox. Figured things out most kids his age wouldn't give a thought.

"How's your day going so far, Bud?" Ramsey's heart smiled.

"I'd be doin' a lot better if you'd let me ride that white mule over there."

"You want to ride old Sara, do you?"

"I was thinkin' if I could learn to hang on to the mule, then when I got big enough to put a foot to stirrup, ridin' a grown horse would be a cinch."

"I believe you've got a point there." Ramsey couldn't contain the grin. He loved watching his son grow and learn. "Come on. We'll give it a go."

Ramsey and Treasure walked to the corral where the mule grazed. "Grab that blanket off the fence, "Ramsey instructed his son. "Stand real still 'til I get Sara tethered."

Rope in hand, he approached the mule, tied a bridle loop around her nose and forehead, then led her to the spot where Treasure waited. He took the blanket the boy held and threw it over the mule's boney back. "Climb up on the railing there, then ease yourself onto her." Ramsey nudged the mule closer to the fence.

"Treasure Keaton Locke, what are you doing?" Cora came running. "Stop, Mr. Locke. He's too small to be riding on an animal not used to carrying weight," she protested.

"He wants to give it a try, Miss Sutton. It's not fitting that his spirit get broke."

"Of course not, but we can let his neck get broken, can we?" Cora walked over and put her hands around Treasure's waist. "Down from there, young man."

"Aww, I want to ride Sara. I can do it, Cora, I know I can."

Ramsey stepped forward. "He's my son, ma'am." He gently removed Cora's hands. "Do you think I'd let him do anything I thought would get him injured? Trust me on this, can you?"

Reluctantly, she conceded and moved aside. Her hand rested on her stomach, and an expression Ramsey couldn't read crept across her face. Fear, he figured.

"Now, boy, settle on her back and let's see if she'll take a liking to you."

Treasure stretched his leg as far over Sara as he could. Ramsey gave him an assist so that he could sit straight middle of the mule. Sara swished her tail but made no indications she was unhappy about the situation.

"I did it, Papa. Look at me, would ya?"

Grinning, Ramsey led the mule away from the fence and into the center of the corral. "I see you, boy. You're sitting mighty proud up there."

"Yes, sir." Treasure glanced back at Cora and waved.

After a couple turns around the corral perimeter, Ramsey returned the mule to the fence. "Climb down now, boy."

"Aw Papa, do I have to?"

"You do. We can give it a turn again tomorrow when I get back from checking the cattle in the west pasture."

"Yes, sir." Treasure put a foot against the fence rail and scooted off the animal. "She's a swell mule, ain't she, Cora?"

"As mules go, I reckon she's as fine as any." Cora scowled at Ramsey.

"Come on, help me carry in the eggs, Treasure. I can't do all the work around here."

Treasure scurried toward the hen house. "Pleasured to, Cora."

"See I told you he'd be all right," Ramsey defended.

"This time, but I still say he's too young, Mr. Locke."

"A boy's gotta grow up faster here in rangeland, Miss Sutton. It's different than living in the city where everything is the same most days. Out here the elements can switch in a heartbeat, and you gotta be able to turn with them, or you'll most likely get knocked down. Or worse."

"I suppose you're right. I just don't like it, that's all."

Again she placed her hand on her belly, her eyes widened.

"Are you feeling poorly, Miss Sutton? You appear a bit pale."

She looked up at him. The fearful expression in her eyes didn't match the words she spoke. "I'm fit, Mr. Locke, been in the sun too long. Best get those eggs in the house." She hurried off to the hens, and with Treasure's help, finished gathering from the nests before they took solace in the house from the heat of the day.

Ramsey held his hand to shade his eyes and gazed at the sky, wondering what was really going through Cora's mind. He figured it'd come to light sooner or later. Things always did. The sun hung a little west of straight over, and he knew this would be Treasure's quiet time. The hour each day when Cora insisted he come inside to sit at the table with a book, or lay on his pallet and rest. Ramsey didn't understand the purpose of this, but he'd pretty much given free rein to Cora raising the kid as she felt best, and so he didn't question it.

The air cooled when the sun settled low on the horizon. The sky streaked with the orange and crimson colors of sunset. Ramsey finished forking clean straw into the stalls for the mule and team horses. Outside, he leaned against the closed barn door and puffed a cigarillo, the slight breeze cooling against his sweat-soaked shirt. He took a long drag, exhaled slowly, watching the smoke dance into the air. This enjoyment was something he'd had to give up doing in the house since Cora arrived. She said smoke lingered and it wasn't in the best interest for

Treasure to breathe, especially at night when he slept. He respected her wishes. He suspected she was right.

A smile raised the corners of his mouth when he saw Cora step out onto the porch. The wind kicked up and blew wayward strands of hair against her face. He wanted to brush them away, hold her cheeks in his hands and kiss those beautiful pink lips. "Damn." His groin tightened again. He sure couldn't let that get noticed.

"Supper's ready, Mr. Locke. Wash up and come in before the meal gets cold." She waved to him.

"Yes, Miss Sutton. On my way."

By the time he got to the cabin, he'd walked off any evidence of his need. He could think of a much better way to be rid of it, but he didn't reckon that was going happen. Cora made no notice of him when he entered, hung his hat on the hook near the door and washed his face and hands at the basin. He was only the man for whom she kept house, ironed clothes and made meals for him and his child. She seemed content in that role with no desire to change it to anything more personal. She'd erected a fence and Ramsey wouldn't cross it, as much as he might want. His body craved a physical release, for sure, but he'd not make love to a woman again when there was no affection between them. And from where Ramsey stood, that was pretty one-sided.

They ate venison roast with potatoes and carrots from the cellar, where they were stored to last through winter.

Cora baked biscuits and made gravy from the meat drippings to spoon over them.

"Sure is good, Miss Sutton. You're an accomplished cook."

"Thank you, Mr. Locke."

Ramsey noticed Treasure sat sullen, picking at his food. "You got something on your mind, boy?"

"Yes, sir, reckon I do."

"Well spit it out, supper time is when a family talks about its problems." Ramsey patted his son on the head.

Treasure looked down at his plate, wiggled his fork in his hand then looked up at his father. "I've been around here a while now, and I was wonderin' if you'd for sure made up your mind. Are you gonna be my papa, or are you gonna send me packin'?"

Ramsey swallowed a mouth full of food, fighting a grin. He knew this was serious to Treasure, and he'd respect that. "You're my son, Bud, my flesh and blood. I didn't know that until you came here a few months back, but Treasure, once I found out, I became your papa, and nothing will ever make it different. Not ever. You clear on that?"

"Yes sir, reckon I am now. Makes me real happy, too." The child's face brightened with his toothy grin.

"Was there something else you wanted to talk about?" Ramsey asked.

The boy turned his attention to Cora. "Got something to ask Cora, if that's all right?"

"Of course, Treasure. You can ask me anything," she responded.

"Well, I know I got a real momma. I remember and all, but she's in heaven now, and I'm thinkin' I need a momma right here, where I am." He hesitated, lowered his gaze, then looked at Cora. "I was wonderin' if you might want to take that on? If'n I could call you momma?"

Seeking Ramsey's approval, Cora glanced at him. He nodded. She returned her attention to the child, placed her hand on his arm. "Treasure, I love you as if you were my child, and I would be most honored to be your *on earth* momma, but only because your real mother can't be with you. Do you understand?"

"Yes'um, that's what I meant."

"Then we're agreed."

"Yes'um. Can I have a piece of that berry pie you baked this mornin', Momma?"

"Finish your carrots, Bud, then you can have pie," Ramsey instructed.

"Do as your father says," Cora followed.

Cora looked across the table at Ramsey and caught him smiling at her. He quickly lowered his eyes and ate the last of the venison on his plate as if regretful he'd offered the facial pleasantry. Again she felt the flutter in her stomach. *Oh, can it be?* She'd never been pregnant, but she was certain she experienced the stirrings of a baby growing inside her. She'd conceived William's child, and he would never know. Cora hadn't given a thought to the fact her woman time hadn't come since she'd left Kansas. She assumed the shock over the loss of her husband, the stress of caring for Berta until her death, and the exhaustive trip to bring Treasure to his father had taken a toll. Calculating now she figured it'd been nearly five months since she flowed and there was no doubt the cause.

She dared a glance at Ramsey. He sopped a biscuit in gravy. She feared he would not be so kind about her staying on when he found out she was with child. He'd taken on more than most men would have, and while their arrangement allowed him to be free of the full responsibility of caring for his son, she was sure his expectation of her role didn't include bringing another child into the picture. How would this unexpected turn of events affect the promise she'd made to Treasure, to be his mother? *Oh, dear.*

Perhaps, now that she carried her father's grandchild, he'd be open to the idea of her coming home. Surely he'd see that in her condition she should be with family. She wouldn't abandon Treasure, though. Arrangements would be made with Ramsey for the child to spend the school year with her, freeing him to work the ranch. Treasure's education would be more advanced in the eastern schools. His father couldn't argue that fact. She would have the child escorted back to Texas to spend summers with his father. She was positive Ramsey would agree. If he needed someone to watch Treasure, she was confident Mrs. Hollister would oblige. That would be the only fair arrangement under the circumstances.

Cora pushed her dilemma aside, got up and started to clear the table. "Everyone ready for a slice of pie?" she asked.

Tomorrow she'd make an excuse to take the buckboard into town and send a telegram to her father. Cora was certain he wouldn't turn his back on her now.

4

Ramsey ate the last of his breakfast eggs, washing them down with a swig of coffee. "I'm riding to the upper Washoo range today. Gotta start bringing the last of the cattle down to the lower pastures. Winter will be hitting on us before much longer. There was frost on the ground this morning."

"I've noticed the nights have cooled a great deal lately." Cora sat a pot of beans on the wood stove to cook for supper. "Time to put extra blankets on the beds."

"And keep the fire stoked at night." Ramsey gulped the last of the dark brew.

"Mr. Locke," Cora said removing her apron. "I'd like to take the buckboard and go into town while you're away if that would be agreeable. We have need of a few staples."

"Of course, get what you need. Tell Fletcher at the Mercantile to put the items on my tab. I'll go in next week and pay up."

"Mrs. Hollister has more than once invited Treasure to come and play with her children. Perhaps I could stop by there on my way, take some slices of the pie I made yesterday, and see if Treasure would be welcome there while I went on into Rabbit Glen," Cora suggested.

"That'd be fine, I reckon. How do you feel about that, Treasure?" Ramsey ruffled his son's hair.

"Supposin' it'd be a right nice thing. I like Henry. Don't care much for his sister, though." Treasure wrinkled his nose.

Ramsey laughed. "I expect Priscilla Hollister isn't too fond of you either, boy. Don't reckon she'll want you underfoot. However, she might be grateful you showed up."

"Why would she?" Treasure puzzled his brow.

"Because you'll keep Henry occupied, so he won't pester her," Cora explained.

"That's right," Ramsey agreed.

Cora busied herself with clearing the table and setting the dishes in the wash pan, filling it with hot water from the kettle on the stove. "It's settled then. Treasure will visit at the Hollisters' while I go into town and get supplies. We'll be back long before you come down out of the hills."

"Reckon so." Ramsey took his hat from the peg near the door, pushed it onto his head, and retrieved his coat from the peg and the rifle from the corner. "Maybe I'll spot a jackrabbit or a pheasant when I'm coming home. Make for a good stew tomorrow."

"Yes, Mr. Locke that would be lovely."

He opened the door, silhouetted by the morning rays. "You need any help hitching the team to the wagon, Miss Sutton?"

"Treasure and I can manage, but thank you for offering," Cora said, turning to face him. Ramsey was a good man. He'd offered her the utmost kindness, and where his son was concerned, he wore his heart on his sleeve. Her stomach did a little dance, but it wasn't the baby's movement this time. Ramsey stood tall, legs splayed, tanned and handsome in the sunlight. Her breath caught. She shouldn't have these kinds of stirrings with her husband barely cold in his grave. Knowing she shouldn't though, didn't keep them from curling around her belly button and shooting an arrow downward.

"Then I'll see you and the boy later this evening." He waved, walked out and closed the door behind him.

It didn't take long for Cora to realize if it weren't for Treasure's knowledge from watching his father hook the horses to the wagon, she'd have never got them hitched. It took longer than she'd hoped, but finally, they climbed to the seat, and she gave the reins a whip. "Yah, gitty up, team."

Twenty minutes later Cora tied the team at the Hollisters'. She and Treasure walked to the door and knocked. When Mary Lou opened the door, Cora spoke her request.

"Why, Cora, we'd be pleased for Treasure to keep Henry company for a while. If you haven't gotten back by lunchtime, don't fret, I'll feed the boy."

"Thank you so much, Mrs. Hollister. I can get my errands done faster without a little one to keep an eye on."

The rotund woman circled as she talked, forcing Cora to turn to continue facing her. "Is there something on my dress?" She asked, thinking perhaps Mary Lou was inspecting her clothing.

A high pitched giggle erupted from the woman. "Oh, no, dear, your dress is lovely. I was noticing that you've filled out some since you've been in Rabbit Glen. I guess having to cook for a hard working man and a growing boy...well, if you cook it, you eat it, right?"

Cora felt her cheeks flame. When she awoke this morning, it was as if her body had made a complete change during slumber. She'd had great difficulty fastening her skirt, and the buttons on her blouse puckered over enlarged breasts.

"I've noticed that myself," she said. "I vowed just this morning to cut my portions in half. That's why I brought the leavings of this apple pie for your family to finish up." Cora hoped her lie sounded credible.

"It'll be enjoyed, I assure you, dear."

Cora gave Treasure a quick hug and climbed to the wagon seat. "I'll be back soon. You be on your best behavior, young man."

"If I promise, maybe you might bring back one of them penny candies I like so much?"

"You'll mind your manners, candy or not, else your papa will take you to the woodshed," Cora warned.

"Yes'um."

She gave the horses their rein, and they started down the road. Cora turned once to wave, then focused on the chore ahead.

"Jesse, I'd appreciate it if my telegram is kept private. Don't need the whole town knowing my business," Cora said, writing out the words she wanted the telegraph operator to send. *Father. I wish to come home. I'm carrying your grandchild. I want you to know each other. When might you be ready to receive me? Your devoted daughter, Cora.*

"I'll be back in town next week. I'll come by then to see if there's a reply," Cora stated. "Please don't give the response to anyone to deliver."

"Yes, ma'am, whatever you say."

"You won't forget, Jesse?"

"No, ma'am, I surely won't."

Cora left the telegraph office and walked down the street to the mercantile. Inside on the counter, she spied the large glass jar filled with colorful, striped candy sticks. The sign on the jar read *2 for a penny*. She picked out four of different colors. Treasure would love this surprise, and she'd give one to Henry and his sister.

"Will that be all for ya?" the young man behind the counter asked.

"I need a can of black tea and a pound of pinto beans," Cora told him. "Oh, and a box of oats."

"I'll get that made up for you. Take just a moment."

"Thank you."

Cora waited, browsing through the bolts of fabric. What she wouldn't give for a new skirt, one that wasn't so tight in the waist. When she returned to her parents' home, perhaps her mother would buy her one. Cora smiled. Her mother loved doting on her when she could do it without her father's notice.

Cora's smile waned.

Her father was a stern man with little tolerance for anything except what was a necessity. Affection and compassion weren't considered priorities in his world. Her parents' marriage was arranged. Her mother remained in the shadows of her existence, hiding from her husband's rage. William was such a kind and loving man, no wonder Cora found it easy to go against her father's demands and marry him. And Ramsey? She had no comparison for the handsome Mr. Locke. He was all any woman might hope for in a husband and father for her children. However, that was a dream Cora didn't expect to come her direction. Ramsey expressed no interest in taking a wife. In taking what she was willing to give. In loving her.

The bell on the door tinkled. Cora looked up to see Minny Perkins and Jenny Ott enter the store. They caught her eye, and she smiled at them.

"Miss Sutton, I've got your order ready," the clerk announced.

Cora returned to the counter and picked up the cotton sack containing her items. Mr. Locke would like you to put this on his tab. He will be in next week to pay up."

"Yes, ma'am. I can do that."

"Oh, Cora, are you in town alone?" Minny placed a hand on her arm, not willing to let her go until she gouged some tidbit of information from her, something she could spread throughout the whole community.

"I am Minny, dear. Treasure is spending time with Henry Hollister, and I'd better be on my way to pick him up before he outlives his welcome." Cora took a step to leave, but Minny tightened her grip.

"And Ramsey, how does he fare these days? We don't see much of him. I don't think he's been to church services once since you arrived. He must be awful tangled up come Sundays." Minny scrunched her nose into one large wrinkle and flared her nostrils.

"Mr. Locke has a ranch to run and a son to care for." Cora jerked her arm away. "Winter is coming, and the cattle have to be moved. I'm sure once all is ready, he'll grace the church again." She was sure if Ramsey was kneeling in prayer in front of the pulpit every day and three times on Sunday it wouldn't be enough to suit Minny Perkins.

Cora walked to the door of the mercantile, paused, and turned back. "You know, Minny, God, doesn't only live within the walls of a church. Look around you. He's everywhere."

Cora opened the door and slammed it shut behind her. She still fumed as she headed the team south, toward the Hollister place. "Nosey old biddy."

Treasure was beside himself when told he could give a candy stick to his friends. "You got one for all of us," he exclaimed. "Henry, come look what we got."

"One for Priscilla, too," Cora reminded.

"I know."

While Treasure passed out the treats, Cora expressed her appreciation to Mary Lou. "Thank you again for letting Treasure play with your children."

"It's good for Henry to have another boy around. He gets rather downtrodden having an older sister boss him all day."

The women laughed.

"Come, Treasure. We best be heading home. Your Papa will want his supper ready when he comes in after a hard day."

"How are you and Ramsey getting on?" Mary Lou inquired, giving a one-sided grin. "You seem in good enough spirits."

Cora felt there was more to the question than was stated. She chose her words carefully.

"It's a good arrangement for both of us. I get room and board, Mr. Locke gets his meals and house looked after, and Treasure has someone to care for him when his father is riding the range."

The reverend's wife arched a brow. "Perhaps the two of you might think about making the arrangement more, shall we say, permanent, all things considered, I mean."

To what *things* was she referring? Cora chose not to take the comment to task. "Treasure, get into the buckboard. Time to go."

She helped the boy to his seat and climbed in beside him. "Thank you again, Mrs. Hollister, for your kindness towards Treasure."

"You really should consider what I said, Cora. A permanent arrangement between you and Ramsey seems in order."

Cora snapped the reins and turned the wagon toward the Lost C. That would be wishful thinking on her part. Ramsey showed no interest in making their arrangement more than it was. No interest in her. At least not in the way Mary Lou suggested.

All the way back to the ranch, Cora had an unsettled gnaw in her belly. Not so much the words Mary Lou spoke, but how she'd said them. There was some underlying meaning, knowing the Reverend's wife as she did. A sudden chill snaked her spine, and she shivered in its cold foreboding.

On Saturday, Ramsey stayed close around the cabin. He spent the better part of the day mending fence in the south section of the ranch to properly contain cattle he'd transferred to that pasture. Cora watched from the kitchen window as he rode into the yard and tied the Appaloosa to the hitching rail. He swung his leg over the saddle to dismount, her breath caught. Levis pulled tight across a muscled, well-proportioned buttocks. The image flamed her cheeks, and a tingle ran circles at the juncture of her legs. Some of the women she'd known in Kansas complained about having to fulfill their wifely duties. She'd nodded when they spoke of their distaste, but she rather enjoyed the coupling act. It was something she missed, and she imagined she and Ramsey might fit together well in that way. *Oh, gracious.* She couldn't allow such thoughts. Carrying another man's child would shove a wedge between her and Ramsey even if there wasn't anything else blocking the way. She'd have to tell him about her situation soon—that she'd be leaving once she got word back from her father and taking Treasure with her if he agreed with the plan.

Looking out the window again, Cora saw Ramsey make a rope halter for old Sara. She watched Treasure climb on her back and spend delightful minutes riding the animal around the yard. He'd gotten quite good at managing the mule.

Treasure halted and yelled to his father, who'd started to walk toward the house. Ramsey turned and gave specific instructions, pointing toward the crabapple tree on top of a nearby hill. "No farther, Treasure. Then you come right back. You hear me, boy?"

The smile on Treasure's face said all that was needed. He nudged Sara's sides, and off they sauntered.

"You think that was a good idea?" Cora asked when Ramsey came into the cabin.

"You gotta give the boy a little rein ever now and again. If you don't, he can't grow...become a man."

"I guess, but I worry."

Ramsey chuckled. "You can see his every move right out the window."

Cora faced Ramsey, hands on her hips. "Yes, I know that, Mr. Locke."

She noticed the smile on his mouth fade. He licked his lips and perused her, his eyes flashed fire. *Oh dear God, he's noticed the changes my body's taken on.* Cora turned quickly to face the kitchen counter again. "You know, Mr. Locke, I fear I must restrain from making dessert so often. I can't discipline myself not to eat some if I bake a pie or cake." She stirred the beans, clanking the lid when she replaced it on the kettle. "I swear I've gained ten pounds since I've come to Rabbit Glen."

Ramsey poured a cup of coffee from the pot on the stove. "I enjoy a woman with a little meat on her bones, Miss Sutton."

"There's a piece of salt pork there on the table," she said, not responding to the comment that weakened her knees and flamed her thoughts. "I brought it in from the smokehouse, but the knife has dulled, and I don't have the strength to push it through. Suppose you could cut a few slices? I'd like to get some in to soak for breakfast in the morning."

Ramsey seemed his usual self when he answered. "Reckon I can. You got a thought on scrambling some fresh eggs to go with it?"

"I do," Cora replied.

"Don't know if I'll be able to sleep tonight, thinking about what's gonna be on the table in the morning."

Hell, it wasn't the thought of food that kept him awake at nights. It was the desire to caress Cora's firm, full breasts that her dress labored to contain. She had put on a few pounds. That pleasured him. He liked a woman with enough rump to swing a leg over on a cold winter night. Although hers was a hip he didn't think he'd be snuggling up to any time in the future. He suspected they'd fit together like a well-oiled cog. Like two people destined for each other. Like two people stirrup over saddle in love.

"I'll ring the bell, get Treasure coming this way. Supper is ready." Cora set a big plate of hot cornbread on the table and went to the door. "I'll dish the beans when he gets in and washed up."

Ramsey finished cutting the pork meat, wrapping the remainder to place back in the smokehouse. Through the open front door, he saw Cora reach to take hold of the bell string and shake it back and forth. Her hips swayed rhythmically. Her body in motion caused him to grow hard. It was a good thing it took her a few minutes to get Treasure's attention. Sure as hell couldn't have her notice the bulge in his jeans.

"That boy," she said. "He's staring off at something like he's in another world." Cora crossed her arms over her breasts and leaned against the porch rail.

"I'll take this salt pork back to the smokehouse." Ramsey held up the wrapped meat. "It'll take the young'un a couple of minutes to get the mule down the hill."

Cora glanced again in Treasure's direction. "I don't think so, Mr. Locke. He's got Sara in a trot, and he's hanging on for dear life. What in the world...?"

"Momma. Papa," Treasure yelled, as he yanked up on the rope that guided the old mule. "Momma, Papa," he shouted again and jumped to the ground as soon as he'd guided the mule into the yard. He stumbled, fell, picked himself up and ran as fast as he could toward the front porch.

Ramsey and Cora rushed to meet him. "What's wrong, son? Did you run into a snake in the bushes?"

Treasure put his hands on his knees, took a second to catch his breath then looked up at his parents, stone-faced serious. "We gotta hurry and get on our Sunday-go-to-meetin' clothes."

"What are you talking about?" Cora asked.

"I seen 'em from atop the hill."

"Saw who?" Ramsey squatted, eye level with his son.

"The preacher, Papa. He's a-comin' and he's bringin' the whole dang choir."

5

"What the hell?" Ramsey witnessed dust billowing into the air from the oncoming team, although the wagon wasn't yet in sight.

"I think I know why," Cora said. She leaned over the porch rail to get a better view.

"Come on inside, and you can share what you think you know." Ramsey hurried everyone into the cabin, shut the door, rested against it, and folded his arms over his chest. "Well?" Eyebrows arched he waited for Cora's explanation.

"When I was in town the other day, I ran into Minny Perkins. Seems she blames me for the fact they haven't seen you in church lately.

"Why would she blame you for that?"

"I believe she thinks I'm taking up your free time on Sunday mornings, engaging you in activities that keep you close to home." Cora blushed.

"I'm sleeping in the barn, for Christ's sake. That woman could make a beehive out of a pea." Ramsey went to the kitchen window and looked out. "They're here. Did Hollister think he had to bring the whole church congregation out here to put a guilt on me?" He turned to Treasure. "Go wash your face and hands, son."

Treasure ran to do as told. Cora straightened her apron and smoothed back her disheveled hair while Ramsey buttoned the top button on his chambray shirt. When the wagon pulled to a stop in the yard, the three walked onto the porch to greet their visitors.

"Good day to you, Reverend," Ramsey called out, tasting grit stirred by the horses' hoofs. "To what do we owe the pleasure of a church visitation?"

The reverend hadn't brought the choir with him, as Treasure thought, but rather his wife, Mary Lou, Minny Perkins and her husband, Jacob. The Ott sisters, Jenny and Rebekah, and the church soloist, Melvin Finch, who'd once sang in a music show with Fanny Harris, whoever that was. Melvin seemed to think the woman's name added prestige to his own. Then there was Mrs. Mahoney whose mouth always looked like she'd eaten sour lemons.

"Good day to you, Ramsey...Cora...Treasure."

The gentlemen helped the ladies from the wagon, and they all stood in a tight bunch like they'd come to attend a wake.

"Hollister, I know I've been lax about getting to church. I need to make sure the boy, Cora and I are in the pew. I'm aware Treasure ought to be exposed to the

Word on a regular basis. Soon as I get my cattle moved down into the lower corral, we'll be coming to services. Next week. I promise."

"Your spiritual well-being and that of Cora and your son, of course, is important, but that's not why we've come, Ramsey."

Mrs. Mahoney made her way to the front of the group. "We've come to see *you* do the right thing by this woman, Mr. Locke." She raised her ample arm and pointed her finger toward Cora.

"Whatever do you mean?" Cora questioned. "Mr. Locke has treated me with nothing but kindness." If panic was a runaway stage, her stomach was the wheel about to fold under. *Oh, God, don't let this be what I think it is.*

"Yes, we can see the results of that," Minny spouted.

Ramsey stepped off the porch onto the staircase and gripped the railing. "Hollister, you want to tell me what this is all about?"

Reverend Hollister cleared his throat. "Seems the women folk in our congregation want you to take responsibility for your actions."

Mrs. Mahoney elbowed the preacher hard and scowled.

"And...er, the menfolk feel the same way," he added.

"What actions would that be, Reverend?" Ramsey clenched his teeth. "I've got no idea what you're rambling on about, and I sure don't appreciate the accusations."

Minny Perkins and Mary Lou Hollister walked over to the porch steps, shaking their fingers. "You've got this woman with child, that's what you've done. You need to marry Cora and make an honest woman out of her," Minny instructed.

"The Lord demands it," Mary Lou ordered.

Ramsey arched a brow, gripped the stair rail. "You'd be speaking the truth if that was the case, but I've not soiled Miss Sutton. There's some mistake, I've never even kissed the woman."

"Miss Sutton, are you going to deny you are carrying a baby in your belly?" Minny shouted.

Cora's hand rested protectively on her stomach. Damn Jesse. He'd told them about her telegram to her father, how else would they know? There was no use lying about her condition. That time had come and gone. "No, Minny, I can't deny it."

"I knew as much." Mary Lou conferred. "All that extra girth around your middle and your...your bosom was a dead giveaway. When Minny saw you coming out of the telegraph office, well, she pried the details from Jesse." Mary Lou slapped her hands together like she won first prize at the county fair hog callin' contest.

Ramsey froze, jaw dropped. He stumbled, stepped backward and pushed the cabin door open. "Treasure, you go on inside. Stay put until I call you."

"But Papa, I wanna know what's going on out here," he protested.

"Inside now, young man." He placed his hand on the boy's shoulder and encouraged him through the doorway.

"I'll go, I reckon."

Ramsey rubbed his hand through his sweat-dampened hair, his eyes fixed and hard. The sound of a bumblebee gathering nectar from the honeysuckle near the porch roared in his ears, like a train about to run him over. He shook his head to bring his mind into focus again.

"Reverend, can you give Cora and me a moment? We'll need to have a talk in the barn."

"Take your time. We ain't goin' nowhere." Reverend Hollister took off his hat, slapped it against his leg to dispel the dust.

"Join me, won't you. Miss Sutton?" Ramsey took hold of Cora's elbow and escorted her off the porch and into the barn, slamming the door shut behind them.

His gaze unwavering, he asked, "You want to explain what the hell these good Christian people are saying, that you confirmed? About you being in a family way?" Ramsey took a close look at the woman standing before him. Hell, he was a damn idiot. If he'd opened his eyes sooner, he'd have noticed the changes in Cora's body weren't due to a few gained pounds. He took a good look. She was beautiful in the way her body expanded to accommodate the child growing inside her. Ramsey wanted to embrace her, tell her everything was going to be all right, protect her, and love her. Too late. He'd loved her for a while now, but carrying the child of her late husband bound Cora to William, not to him.

Cora lowered her head unable to meet his gaze. "I said I can't deny it." She stood silent a moment before she raised her lashes to stare into Ramsey's eyes. "I was going to tell you."

"And when were you thinking of doing that? You should have mentioned it when you first came, might have changed my offer to let you stay."

She placed her hand on his arm. "I...I...."

He jerked away. Clenched his fist.

"I haven't deceived you, Ramsey." Cora brushed a tear from her cheek. "I was with child when I got here, but I was oblivious to any signs indicating my condition. With Berta and William's deaths, the exhaustive long trip to Rabbit Glen, I figured the reason my body wasn't doing its...its...woman thing was from fatigue." She took a deep breath. "It wasn't until I felt the flutter in my belly that I suspected." Cora's cheeks flamed, and she pressed her palms to her face.

"So what the hell are we going to do now? That's a lynch mob out there."

Cora sat on a bundle of straw. "I'm so sorry I brought this to your door, Mr. Locke. You have treated me well. You don't deserve to have your reputation blackened in this way. I will tell them it's not your baby, but rather my dead husband's." She tilted her head upward, smiled. "I've sent a telegram to my father requesting assistance to return home."

Ramsey sat next to her. "With what you've told me about your father, do you think there's any hope he'll allow that?"

"How could he deny me? Surely he wants to know his grandchild. That would motivate him to welcome me back."

"I think that's a slim thread to count on." Ramsey ran his hand through his hair again. "Here's how I see it, Miss Sutton. Most likely your father isn't going to favor your return, especially if you're carrying the child of the man who stole you away from him and his vision for your life. For the sake of argument, let's say he agreed. Have you given a thought to how your leaving would stir up Treasure's life?" Ramsey asked.

"I was hoping to take him to live with me during the school year, the months where you spend most your days working cattle, making sure they winter well. He'd receive an excellent education, more advanced than in a small town school. He could spend summers with you. You could schedule your work days closer to home. If you needed assistance, I'm sure Mary Lou Hollister would step in to help."

"My son was jerked away from the only life he knew when his mother died. Now he's found a new way of being, he's settled, happy, and I'm not about to have that taken from him again."

Tears slid down Cora's cheeks. "I love Treasure, I would do nothing to hurt him, but what choice do I have? This situation is not what you bargained into, Ramsey."

"I've got a thought on the matter if you'd care to hear it."

"Of course, I'll listen to any suggestion that might reconcile our present dilemma," she said.

"Treasure will stay with me, no discussion on that score. He's my son, and I've grown to love him more than my next breath." *And I've grown to love you, Cora. I want to tell you, but now...well....*

However, the fact remains that I do need someone to watch over him when I'm herding cattle from one grazing range to another, and when I'm working in the high country, away from the cabin for days at a time. Treasure cares about you. My God woman, he wants you to be his momma. You staying on is an answer for both of us, me and Treasure, like it or not." Ramsey's heart constricted with the possibility that Cora would choose to leave. Blood pooled in his temples and throbbed like an anvil against hot steel.

"I never said I didn't like the arrangement, Mr. Locke, but there's going to be a baby in a few months, that I can't change. Another mouth to feed."

Ramsey smiled. "I don't reckon a little thing like that could eat much, and you'd be the feed bucket for a long while anyhow."

"True, but what of the church folks and their accusations? It's not right, Mr. Locke. You should not be required to take responsibility for an act you didn't commit."

"Miss Sutton, I don't think Jesus Christ himself could convince that bunch out there I'm not the daddy of that baby growing inside you. They got their calendars out, and it all added up to them. No changing their minds."

"But...."

Ramsey laid a gentle finger against Cora's lips. "I see only one way out of this. Get married, as they want. You'd stay on and take care of Treasure and the house duties as you've been doing. It'd be a matter of me giving you my name, that's all."

"Your name? Nothing more?"

Ramsey pressed to make her understand he'd ask nothing of her she wasn't ready to give. "We'd be married on paper, but the arrangement between us would stay as it is. I wouldn't ask you to fulfill any wifely obligations if that's what worries you, but us getting married seems the best tack under the circumstances. The church ladies could then rest a respectful eye upon you and the baby, once it comes. No hurtful words would fall on Treasure's ears, and I'd still be in good graces because I did right by you. To make things right in the eyes of the church you'd be required to take my name. Would that be so difficult for you to accommodate?"

Cora sighed and rubbed her sweaty palms against her skirt. "I...I don't know, Mr. Locke, it's seems so unorthodox."

"Maybe so, but I do think it's the best approach to our situation. Treasure and that little one you carry are the priority here, not you or me." *We can make this work, Cora. I know we can.*

"You make a valid point, Mr. Locke. I believe, under the circumstances, I can agree to what you propose. You're sure you're willing?"

"I'd be agreeable to it, Miss Sutton." *So damn agreeable.* Maybe it wasn't the best reason to marry, but he'd take it, and hope someday in the future Cora would find a place for him in her heart? Maybe she'd come to love him? Maybe.

Cora simply nodded her head. Her shoulders sagged. Why did her heart ache so with disappointment? She was grateful Ramsey was willing to take her as his wife, salvage her reputation, and continue to give her a place to live, so she wouldn't have to leave Treasure. Cora appreciated all these things, but she wanted more than a marriage of convenience.

"Let's go give the Reverend and his mob our decision." Ramsey opened the barn door and led the way back to the group. Cora followed close behind.

"Reverend, Miss Sutton and I can see the error of our ways and the wisdom of your words. We'd like you to marry us. We'll come to the church next Sunday prepared to take our vows."

Minny Perkins clapped her hands and did a jig in the dirt. "Hallelujah!"

Mary Lou raised her arms to the sky. "Praise the Lord," she offered. This was followed by similar accolades to the powers above from others in the crowd.

"Got the paper right here. Make you all nice and legal before the sun goes down." Reverend Hollister pulled a black folder from his coat pocket.

"Now? You want to do the wedding right now?" Panic poured from Cora's skin. "I'm not cleaned up, and my hair's a mess. Surely you don't expect me to get married in this state?"

"No better time to fix a mistake than the moment you know you made one." Reverend Hollister walked up the steps to the porch. "I'll stand here, and you and Cora come up and stand right there in front of the window. Have ya hog-tied 'fore you know what happened."

Ramsey glanced at Cora and raised a brow. "Think the Reverend is dead-set on his intention to get us married today. Doubt we can convince him different."

"No. I don't think we can." Cora removed her apron, and smoothed her hair with her hand, tucking a loose strand into the bun at the back of her head. She pinched her cheeks to bring some color; sure she looked as pale as a ghost. Her head was spinning as though she was dream walking.

Ramsey grasped Cora's arm, and they climbed the steps to the porch. "Wanna get my boy." Ramsey turned toward the cabin door, opened it. "Treasure, come here."

The child stood next to his father and tugged at his shirt sleeve. "Why'd the preacher come, Papa? Are we in trouble? Did we break a *comandent*?"

"We're not in trouble, son. Cora and I have decided to get married. Would you like that?"

"Oh, yes, sir. I think that'd be as fine as a candy stick with red stripes." The boy's face glowed like a candle at midnight.

"Find a spot to stand between us, Treasure. You need to be a part of the ceremony, too." Ramsey moved so Treasure could squeeze into place. "Reckon we're ready, Reverend."

This wasn't the wedding Cora envisioned if, in fact, there was a second marriage for her. She'd hoped one day she and William might have the lavish wedding she'd dreamed of as a child. She'd wear a white ruffled dress with her bridesmaids dressed in pale green. Their short ceremony by the court clerk made their union legal, and William promised she would have her fancy wedding one day in the future. His death put an end to their plans. Cora held to the dream, though. *At twenty-three, wasn't there still time for her to fall in love again?* Her vision of walking the church aisle in a flurry of rose petals waned. Instead, here she was, getting married a second time in a rushed and forced ritual to a man she hardly knew. There been no affection expressed between her and Ramsey, nothing to bring them to this juncture in life. It wasn't at all what she'd hoped. Her heart cried the tears her eyes would not shed.

Cora blocked out the words Reverend Hollister spoke, until the part where he said, "All right now, Ramsey, you may kiss your bride."

She stood paralyzed. Ramsey lowered his head, and she felt his breath on her cheek as he moved to press his lips against hers. Tender at first, then with a hunger she didn't want to deny. He wrapped her in his arms, pulled her body to meet his obvious need and she responded. Her mouth parted to receive the teasing of his tongue. She pressed her swollen breasts against his chest, her fingers buried in his straight dark hair.

As unexpectedly as the passion had overtaken them, it ended when Ramsey pushed her away, his eyes ablaze with anger. Damn him. He blamed her for what had happened between them. She could see it reflected in those steel gray eyes, hard as coal.

Yes, she'd responded, yielded to her feelings, lost herself in the scent of him, wild and earthy. Regardless of his accusing glare, she refused to accept responsibility for the encounter. He could put the fault for it in his pocket. It was him who initiated the kiss. Cora matched Ramsey's stare until he looked away. *If this was an omen to the way their married life would play out, then Ramsey Locke was up against a fierce contender.*

Cheers went up from the onlookers. "Now we know why she got in that condition," Mr. Perkins joked. "I bet this old cabin will be on fire tonight, and we know who'll be strokin' the match."

The men in the group roared.

"You're not drinking with your cronies, Jacob Perkins. We'll have no such talk in the presence of ladies," Mary Lou scolded.

Ramsey's head stopped spinning, and he sobered. What the hell had happened? He'd only meant to give Cora a little peck on the side of her mouth, make the marriage official and all, but the second his lips touched hers, he was a goner. Her body melted against him. Her breasts against his chest brought him to the pinnacle of desire. Desire to take her to his bed. Desire to bury himself in her warmth. Desire to make her his wife in every way. He'd fallen hard and it'd only taken Cora's smile and her strength to pull him in. *The trouble was, it appeared a one direction road.*

He shook his head, dislodging the thoughts that inflamed him. Cora agreed to a marriage in name only. He'd promised to demand no intimacy between them, assured Cora on that score. He wished he could take those words back, make her see they'd fit together like berries and cream. Too late to mend that bridge now. *Dammit.*

6

The Reverend and Mrs. Hollister couldn't hide their elation when Cora, Ramsey, and Treasure walked into the church for Sunday service. "Nice to see all my sheep back in the fold." The Reverend stated from behind the pulpit.

"Find a seat in the back, so we can make a quick escape once this is over," Ramsey whispered. He ushered Cora to a pew, put Treasure between them, and they all sat. It seemed to Ramsey the sermon went on unduly long this particular Sunday. The Reverend spouted about the rages of sin, the need to cleanse one's soul. He looked toward Ramsey when he spoke, as if to convey, *you're all clear on that score, now you've done the honorable thing with Cora.*

Treasure squirmed in the seat and twisted his fingers together. Cora patted his knee, understanding the child's impatience. She adjusted her too-snug jacket and squared her shoulders.

Finally the last amen was given. Ramsey and his family hurried outside, but before they could get to the wagon and climb on, they were surrounded by well-wishers. The men shook his hand, the ladies congratulated Cora and hugged Treasure, which by his facial expressions he didn't care for much.

"Cora and I thank you all for your acceptance of our new-formed family, and we hate to run off, but we must to get to town and purchase some items at the mercantile. Don't want to be on the road going home after dark." Ramsey picked up his son and sat him in the back of the buckboard, then helped Cora climb onto the seat.

"We got a parcel of heathens in town keepin' their establishments open on the Sabbath. Not much better is the man who shops their wares on the Lord's day," Reverend Hollister judged.

"I think God Almighty will make an exception this time, Reverend, seeing I've got a pregnant wife and a young'un and no staples in the cupboard," Ramsey countered. He glared at the minister for a long moment before climbing into the wagon next to Cora.

"I suppose you could be right about the Lord's forgiveness of ya doin' business today, your circumstances what they are." Reverend Hollister removed his signature beaver skin hat and wiped his brow. "See you folks next Sunday, will I?"

"Reckon you will," Ramsey replied, his heart not in it.

Ramsey pulled the wagon to a stop near the blacksmith shop, got out and came around to assist Cora from her seat.

She smoothed the skirt of her dress. "You and Treasure go on to the general store, Ramsey. I'll make a stop at the telegraph office, see if anything came in from my father."

"Why torture yourself, Cora, knowing how your father feels?"

"He might have had a change of heart with the knowledge he's going to have a grandchild." She looked up at him, hope in her eyes. "Besides, I want to give Jesse a scolding for talking out of turn."

"All right, but don't be long. I do want to get home before dark."

"Can I get a candy stick, Momma?" Treasure tugged at Cora's arm.

"If it's agreeable with your father, I have no objection to one candy."

"One's better than nothin', ain't that right, Papa?"

Ramsey draped his arm across the boy's shoulders. "Reckon so." They headed toward the mercantile.

Jesse sat at his desk keying a message when Cora walked in. She crossed her arms on the counter and waited until he'd finished. "So what does it take for you to keep something confidential when you're specifically asked to do so, Jesse Waller?"

"Honest, Miss Cora, I didn't tell nobody nothin'."

"Then how do you explain that the ladies at the church knew of my condition? I never spoke of it except in the telegram I sent."

Jesse licked his lips and cocked his head like he had a kink in his neck he couldn't rid. "It was Minny Perkins. It wasn't more than a minute after you left she stormed in here. I was still standing at the counter, hadn't even sat down to key the message."

"That doesn't explain how she knew information I hadn't given out."

"Ma'am, she jerked the paper you'd written your message on from my hand and read it, every last word." I tried to get it back from her, but she said she'd yell rape if I came closer. What was I to do?"

Cora could see Jesse's dilemma. "Under the circumstances, I guess there was nothing to be done, but there should be a law against such behavior."

"And who in this town would stand up against Minny Perkins?" Jessie asked. "Nobody I know."

"So it's that way? I suppose if the old biddy is determined to stick her nose in another's business, I reckon she'll find a way. Especially if no one is slapping her hands."

"Minny sure will." Jesse stepped up to the counter. "I'm real sorry if she caused you any distress. She has a way of stirrin' up a slop pot."

"Not your fault, Jesse. It all worked out in the end. Ramsey and I are married now. Treasure has an entire family with parents who love him."

"A boy surely needs that, Miss Cora."

She turned to leave then remembered why she'd stopped by in the first place. "Did a reply come?"

Jesse dropped his gaze to the floor. "Yes ma'am, you got a message back." He went to a row of cubbyholes and pulled a yellow paper from one, delivered it to Cora. "Sorry, Miss Cora, real sorry."

"Thanks." Cora stuck the message into her skirt pocket. Jesse's reaction said it all. Her father's reply had not been favorable. She'd read it later when she was alone, where no one would see her tears. Her circumstances had changed now, that was a fact, but her heart ached for her father's love. For his forgiveness.

Cora left the telegraph office heading toward the mercantile to catch up with her husband and son. She saw Ramsey standing outside in conversation with Rusty McAllen and Shorty Brennan. The men waved their hands in the air, pointed to the east as they talked. Ramsey stood and listened. From her distance, she couldn't hear the words but gathered it was something the two men thought would interest Ramsey. They'd disbanded by the time she arrived at the store. Inside she found Ramsey and Treasure checking out rancher hats.

"Getting a new head cover, are you, Ramsey?" she asked.

"Nope. Mine serves me well." He tapped the brim of his black felt. "The boy thinks he needs one before winter sets in."

"Your son is smart. It's hard to get out and do chores when the snow is blanketing your scalp." Cora ruffled Treasure's hair.

"I want a black one, jus' like Papa's."

"Well, I can't see it any other way," Cora agreed.

Ramsey placed the one Treasure favored on his head. "How's that one meet your fancy?"

Treasure and Ramsey grinned at each other in the round mirror hanging on the wall. Cora couldn't help but smile. The way their mouths curled was exactly the same. Two berries off the same bush.

Treasure eyed himself in the small round mirror. "Reckon this 'un sits mighty fine."

"Chester, how much for this hat?" Ramsey held it up for the clerk to see.

"That one's three dollars and a quarter."

"That's a might high, isn't it?"

Chester sauntered over a toothy grin on his face. "That one came in from a manufacturer in New York, had to pay the shipping to get it here, you know."

"Well, do you have any that didn't come from so far away?" Ramsey asked.

"How 'bout these straws?" Chester picked up a tan hat with a narrow red band. "That's all we got for the time. Should be gettin' more hats in after Thanksgiving."

Treasure's mouth pouted, his eyes dimmed. "I sure had my heart hankerin' on a black hat, like this'un."

"Over three dollars is a lot of money to spend on head cover, boy. I could swing for one of these handsome looking straws. How'd that be?"

Treasure pulled the hat off his head and replaced it on the counter. "I reckon I don't need one." He wandered off to another part of the store. His shoulders drooped under the weight of his disappointment.

Cora's heart broke. Treasure was a sweet child, well behaved and not demanding. He did his chores without fuss, and there was little if anything done to spoil him, except for an occasional candy stick. "Ramsey, hear me out on this before you say anything." Cora rested her hand against his arm, then pulled it away. "Berta gave me some money to make the trip here, to bring Treasure to you. I watched every penny, not knowing how our journey would end up. If you'd let us stay or not."

"And how does that pair up with a three dollar and a quarter hat?" Ramsey placed one booted foot in front of the other, hip cocked and waited to hear the point Cora attempted to make.

"I didn't spend all that money. I've got twelve dollars left. Why couldn't we use a portion of that and get the hat Treasure most desires? I think it'd please Berta."

"That'd be spoiling the boy, don't you think? You can't always have everything you hanker for in life. That's a lesson to learn."

Cora looked up at him, her eyes pleading. "Ramsey, what has the child ever asked? For the two of us to be his momma and papa, nothing more. He doesn't complain that his pants are getting too short or his shirts too tight. All he wants is a hat like the one his daddy wears. I'd be in favor of him having it."

"You're right, Cora. I can see I still got some learning to do on this parenting thing." Ramsey rubbed the back of his neck. "I'll make you a deal."

"What is it?"

"You pay a dollar and a quarter, and I'll cover the rest. This way, I'm putting out what I was willing to spend in the first place, and you'll still have most of the money Berta gave you left. I reckon you'll need to buy some cotton print pretty soon, make yourself some bigger skirts as the baby grows." He glanced toward the window; his jaw tightened with talk of Cora's baby. A baby that wasn't his, but in his heart, he wished it so.

"It's a deal." Cora pulled money from of her purse and handed it to Ramsey. "How thoughtful of you to consider my upcoming needs, Mr. Locke."

Ramsey took the bill and coin and shoved it into his pocket. He glanced around to see if anyone was in earshot. "Don't you think we could drop the Mr. Locke and Miss Sutton now? We're married after all. We live in the same house, we're raising a young'un together, and they'll be another one to look after soon. Reckon it's time we called each other by our first names."

The corners of Cora's mouth stretched, she turned her head. "I could agree to that consideration."

Ramsey spotted the joy she tried to hide. His heart swelled seeing her happy.

"Then it's settled?"

"Yes."

Ramsey strolled away to find Treasure, the black hat in his hand. "Boy, where are ya? Better come fetch this hat before someone else wants to buy it."

Treasure raced to his father's side from behind the saddle tack. "You gonna let me have it, after all, Papa?"

"Cora and I decided it'd be a fitting investment." Ramsey shoved the hat on the boy's head and adjusted the brim. "One thing, though."

"Yes, sir, what's that?"

"You can't allow your head to grow any. This hat's got to last until you've finished with all your schooling."

"I reckon that won't be no hard chore." Treasure assured. "I'll just tell my brain not to take in too much learnin' and my head will stay the same size."

Ramsey belly laughed. "Reckon that'll work, son."

Cora joined them. "I think we might make an exception, Treasure. If your head swells because you're acquiring knowledge, that'd be the only reason we could entertain buying you another hat before you turn sixteen."

Cora and Ramsey were still laughing when they paid for the hat at the counter.

Treasure stood on the walkway staring at the two adults, his eyebrows arched.

"What's climbed your tree, young man?" Cora stooped at the waist to search Treasure's eyes.

"I reckon I've see cows act up same as you two when they got into the loco weed, but I didn't see any of that on the breakfast table."

"Did you miss out on that, son?" Ramsey said.

"Yes, I'm sure I mixed some into the gravy." Cora chuckled.

They all walked down the wooden sidewalk giggling.

"I'm so happy my heart's jumpin' in my chest like popcorn in a hot skillet." Treasure shouted. "I got a momma and a papa, a dang nice new hat, and I belong somewhere."

Ramsey circled one arm around Treasure's shoulder, the other around Cora's waist. "As families go, I'd say we make a mighty fine example."

"Yep, and I got a good friend named Henry, and I got a mule named Sara. What more could a fella ask for? Ain't that right, Papa?"

"I reckon you've got a pretty sweet life," Ramsey told him. *The only thing lacking in my sweet life is the love of a gentile woman.* He patted the side of Cora's expanding waist, where his hand rested against her. *This woman.*

"My life is sure a lot sweeter with you in it, Treasure." Cora left Ramsey's arm and leaned down to kiss Treasure's cheek.

Treasure hugged Cora around the waist. "I love you, momma."

Riding in the back of the buckboard, Treasure scooted on his knees up behind the seat. He set his new hat firm on his head and clamped one hand to the backrest. "Papa, I ain't dreamin' all this am I?"

"You're surely wide awake, son."

"Does all this land far as I can see belong to you?"

"It belongs to all of us, Treasure. You, me and Cora, now that we're married."

"I reckon one day when I've growed, I'll be a sittin' astride a fifteen-hands gelding, instead of old Sara. I'll be helpin' you move cattle from one grazin' pasture to the next. And, I'll be makin' sure them corrals is fixed too."

"That day isn't nearly as far off as you think, Treasure." Ramsey turned and smiled. "Before you know it you'll be my right-hand man, riding alongside, helping me run the Lost C Ranch."

"I'll make ya proud, Papa. I promise. Ya can bet a nickel on that."

They traveled the remainder of the journey in silence. Cora hummed as they rode along. Ramsey thought it a happy tune. Together they'd watch Treasure grow into the man he wanted to be. Watch the new babe take on a life for itself. The years would pass by, and they'd grow old sitting across the table from one another. Perhaps somewhere between now and then he'd convince Cora he'd loved her from nearly the first day she'd stepped foot on the Lost C Ranch. Perhaps somewhere along the way, she'd come to love him too.

7

"*I*'m takin' the buckboard into town this morning," Ramsey said.

Cora set a plate of biscuits on the table and went to dish up a bowl of gravy. "Oh?"

"Gonna pick up supplies." Ramsey smeared butter on the hot bread.

"We got everything we needed when we were in town last week. I'm not short on anything." She brought the bowl to the table and sat.

"Hand me your plate, son." Cora spooned the brown gravy over a split biscuit and added two slices of fried pork meat. "Eat up, Treasure, so you'll grow strong like your papa."

Ramsey smiled. "Think that'll do it, do you?"

"Actually, he doesn't need a reason to eat, or haven't you noticed?"

"I have."

"Is that why you think we need to bring in extra supplies?" Cora asked.

Ramsey took a couple of bites and leaned back in his chair. "Rusty and Shorty are coming back with me. They'll be staying a few days, help get some work done around the place. You'll need to put on a hardy breakfast and supper for those boys."

"I see. Well, of course, that won't be a bother. I'll get a kettle of beans on to cook right away, so they'll be ready for the evening meal."

"Reckon, that'd be good. Put a few chunks of the salt pork in them."

"Yes, I was planning to. It always adds flavor."

Treasure held out his plate for seconds. "If we're gettin' company, Momma, where are they gonna sleep? I got the floor and papa's got the barn."

Ramsey patted his son on the top of the head. "Don't fret on it, boy. All Rusty and Shorty need is a soft spot in the hay, and they'll do fine."

"We should be back a little after noon, I reckon. What do you plan to busy yourself doing today?" Ramsey wasn't good at making small talk, but it seemed the right thing to do when the three of them shared a table.

Cora smiled. "I'm surprised you're interested, but since you asked, I was planning to cut that dark blue cotton I got at the mercantile and gather it into a new skirt. I'll do that while the beans are cooking. Treasure can fetch the eggs this morning."

"Looks like everything's covered. I'll have one more cup of coffee and be on my way." Ramsey filled his cup from the pot and stood at the counter to drink it. When he'd finished, he took his hat off the nail and opened the door. "You mind your momma while I'm gone, you hear me, young'un?"

Treasure looked up at his father. "I always mind her Papa. I ain't hankerin' to get no whuppin'."

Ramsey chuckled. "You've not been punished once, as I recall since you arrived at the Lost C, son. And if I know Cora like I think I do, it isn't likely you'll ever know a spanking." He waved his hand, left out the door, and shut it behind him.

Cora watched from the kitchen window until she could no longer see Ramsey in the wagon, as he headed toward Rabbit Glen. She missed his company. There weren't many days when Ramsey hung around the cabin, doing chores that needed done. On those rare days, they laughed together, interacted with Treasure as he did his assigned tasks. If she didn't think about it too hard, they seemed a real family. It was at night when Ramsey headed to the barn to sleep and she to the bedroom in the house, that she was jolted back to reality.

The morning passed. Treasure pulled seven eggs from beneath the hens and put them in a basket on the counter. He folded his pallet from the floor and stacked it neatly in the corner then grabbed the broom, went outside and swept the porch.

"Momma, I got all my chores done, can I ride Sara for a bit?"

She'd gotten used to seeing the child astride the mule, and they seemed to have a mutual understanding. Treasure didn't kick Sara in the sides, and she didn't buck. "Stay right out front in the yard where I can see you. Understand?"

"Yes 'um." He ran out of the house.

"Sara. Sara, come here girl," he shouted. He placed the rope halter over the mule's head and led her to the fence and climbed on. "We can't go far, old girl, gotta stay close to the house in case momma might need me."

The mule's ears perked up, listening to her rider, as though she comprehended every word. "I don't know much a'tal about women havin' babies, but momma looks like she might fall right over with her belly so big. Since Papa's away, it'd be up to me to pick her up and set her straight if'n she tumbled."

Treasure nudged Sara in the side, and she moseyed around the garden. "We're a good pair, you and me. I don't reckon there's nothin' we couldn't get done that was needin' doin'." He reached down and patted the mule on the neck. "I love you, Sara."

Cora smiled hearing Treasure's comments to his four-legged friend. That's what real love looked like. She sat at the table and began work on her new skirt. She took two rows of running stitches and gathered it up to fit her waist, adding a couple of extra inches. Then fashioned a waistband from the remaining fabric and hand sewed it into place, allowing for an overlap of the band so she could let it out as needed. She added three buttons and three buttonholes. Surely this would give her enough girth room as her belly grew.

She rested her hand on her stomach, the baby moved. Her waistline grew more each day, her condition evident. Would she feel different, more excited if this was Ramsey's child? If they'd met earlier, married and made this baby? A tingle of desire stung her womanhood, embellished the image her mind created. She sighed, shook the want away. It would never be like that between her and Ramsey, and wishing wouldn't make it so.

Ramsey didn't want a wife. He wanted a mother for his child. He'd been willing to give her his name to protect her reputation and to keep unkind talk from reaching Treasure's ears. That said, he was a decent man, but one who didn't want a real marriage all the same.

Two more stitches and her project was complete. Cora laid the fabric aside and looked out the window to check on Treasure. He sat on Sara, talking to her, rubbing her neck. The mule ambled in a circled around the yard in front of the cabin. Knowing her son was in good stead, she went to the sleeping room and slipped out of her extremely too tight skirt, and stepped into the newly sewn garment. "Much better." She took a deep breath, happy to find the waistband didn't cut into her flesh. She left her blouse hanging out. The buttons pulled a little over her breasts, but still, she looked presentable.

Folding the old skirt she had a thought. This cabin would certainly feel more like a home with curtains over the windows. This garment could be sacrificed. Once the baby was born, she could take up the new blue skirt to fit her figure once it got back to normal. She grabbed the scissors and began cutting. Within an hour she had strips of material with small tunnels sewed in the tops, enough for each window. Now, she'd have to figure out how to hang them. There were no curtain rods.

At the front door, Cora yelled, "Treasure, put Sara in the corral and come in for lunch."

"Yes'um. I was gettin' a might starved." He slid off the mule's back.

Cora prepared a lunch of leftover biscuits, butter and jam, and a slice of jerked meat. "I have a job for us after we eat. Are you up to help me?" she asked Treasure.

"What kind of job, Momma? Will it break my back?"

"I doubt you need to worry about that. I thought we might take a walk down to the creek, cut a few of those cottonwood saplings that grow near where the underground spring comes out of the rock."

"I reckon that'd be an easy task, 'specially after I've gobbled down another one of these biscuits with apple jam."

Amusement danced across Cora's mouth as she split a biscuit and slathered it with jam. She waited until he'd licked his lips and drunk his water. "Come on. I want to get down there and back before your papa, and our guests get here."

They found the spot and Cora cut the one inch round saplings with the hand saw she'd retrieved from the barn. Measuring with a piece of string she'd placed against the window to get the distance across, she again cut pieces of wood and stacked them in place. When she had all she needed, five in total, she gave two to Treasure to carry. "We have enough." Cora led the way through the narrow trail. "Look, son, you see that dark green leafed vine with berries?" She pointed to a growth beyond the path.

"Sure, Momma. It's purdy, isn't it?"

"Yes, but It's more than pretty, Treasure. It's a powerful healing remedy if you get a wound. A woman back in Kansas told me about it."

"I'll put that in my head, so I don't forget."

Cora chuckled. "That's a right good plan."

Inside the cabin, she ran a sapling through the tunnel at the top of each strip of fabric she'd sewn. Using a step stool, Cora stood at the window in the sleeping room. She'd made this curtain long enough to hang to the bottom sill so the room could be darkened for when the baby napped during the day.

Once a nail was hammered into the wood on each side of the window, extended out two inches, she carefully positioned the sapling with the curtain attached to rest upon the nails. "Perfect. What do you think Treasure?"

"Sure purdys up the place. You did a mighty fine job sewing 'em, Momma."

"Thank you, kind sir," she said, moving the footstool to the window at the rear of the cabin.

"Can I have that last biscuit, Momma, and go sit on the fence and watch for Papa to come home."

"How can you still be hungry, after that big lunch?"

"Got the same problem as Henry, I reckon."

Cora walked over to Treasure, put her hand on his shoulder. "What problem is that, son?"

"Hollow leg. That's what Mrs. Hollister says Henry has, 'cause he's wantin' to eat somethin' all the time. Guess that's what I've got too."

Cora laughed out loud. "I'd say you might be right on that score." She plucked the biscuit off the plate and handed it to him. "Go. Watch for your father."

Treasure hurried out. "I'll holler when I see 'em."

Cora checked the pot of beans cooking on the stove. She stirred them and tasted. "A bit more salt." She always let them cook a couple of hours without adding salt. When they simmered with pork meat, sometimes that added enough flavor—but these, she decided, were in need of a little boost. Cora put the lid on the kettle, stoked the fire and returned to her task of hanging curtains.

She'd made valances to hang above the kitchen windows. It would allow light into the house as the days became shorter, and there were fewer rays of sunshine. When she was ready to hang curtains over the two windows in the kitchen area, one that looked out to the front yard, and the other toward the chicken coop, she realized even standing on the footstool she couldn't reach high enough to hammer the nails into place or hang the rod.

Cora tucked the hem of her skirt into the waistband and stepped on the stool. She put her knee on the counter and wiggled her way on top, balanced on the narrow ledge. She reached down and grabbed the hammer and nails.

Lovely. Cora admired the hominess the curtains provided.

She took a few careful steps on the countertop and positioned herself in front of the last window, her right foot barely on the counter where it angled into the corner. She held a nail in her left hand and pulled back the hammer to hit it into the wood.

"What the hell are you doing, woman?"

The voice, even though she recognized it, startled her. She turned to look at Ramsey, and her expanding bulk threw her off balance. "Ohhhhh." Cora tumbled from the counter toward the floor. Instinctively she cradled her stomach in her hands.

Ramsey raced toward Cora. His outstretched arms caught her, but the angle at which she fell made it impossible to maintain his balance, and they both fell to the floor. Ramsey's right leg was pinned beneath Cora, which helped to cushion her fall.

"Are you all right? Did you hurt yourself?" He asked, holding her in his arms.

"I didn't hear the wagon come in." Cora rubbed the back of her head.

"We pulled in behind the barn. I walked up to the house." He placed his hand protectively upon her stomach. "The baby...is the baby okay?"

"Thanks to you, I didn't hit all that hard." She rested her hand on his arm. "We both appear to be in good stead."

Ramsey pulled his leg free and squatted on his knees. "What were you doing climbing on the counter that way? Don't you know you could have killed yourself if I hadn't come in when I did."

"If you hadn't been here, Mr. Locke, I wouldn't have fallen. When you shouted it scared me, and that caused the disaster."

"Oh, I'm Mr. Locke again?" Ramsey chuckled. "I can see your point. I supposed I could have spoken a little softer."

Cora couldn't pull her gaze away from his dark fiery eyes. They searched hers as if waiting for an answer—a signal of sorts. Then he leaned close, his parted lips a breath from hers.

She knew what he was about to do, and she had no want to stop him. When his lips touched hers, tender at first, then urgent and wanting, she responded like a drowning critter grasping for a floating log. She reveled in the taste of him, sweet and salty at the same time. His fresh soap smell engulfed her. Filled her. Elevated her to a place she'd never been. Her arms felt natural around his waist and neck. She could get used to this.

Ramsey pulled her close, fused her to him. She parted her lips to welcome his teasing tongue. His hand found the hem of her blouse and pushed beneath it. He cupped her swollen breast, waiting, hidden beneath her camisole. She wanted him to rip away the thin fabric, to feel her flesh bare against his palm—to have his mouth taste her. She trembled, leaned into his caress.

He jerked his hand away, pulled his lips from hers. "What the hell was I thinking?"

"I'm sorry. I never should've done that."

Ramsey got to his feet and helped Cora to a chair. He rubbed his hands against his jean-clad thighs, then rubbed them through his hair and looked away. "Tell me how you want that last curtain hung."

One minute she and Ramsey were in a passionate embrace, and the next he acted as though their shared intimacy was a figment of her imagination. Cora was confused, hurt if truth be known. She wasn't going to let Ramsey see her heartache. He'd made a mistake, said as much. Kissing her, touching her was an error in judgment on his part. She'd have to accept it, respect the boundaries he set forth. The problem was, he'd started a fire in her belly, and she didn't think there was any way to put it out, except to have him kiss her again, run his hands over her body, fill her with his warmth—make her his wife in every way.

"You want it hung like this other one?" Ramsey asked again, not looking at her.

"Yes, that'll do nicely. Thank you."

He hammered the nails and placed the sapling rod. Jumping down from the counter, he stood and admired Cora's handy work. "Looks real nice. Makes the place homey."

Ramsey flipped the hammer in his hand. "I'll take this back to the tack room. Reckon you better get some cornbread into the bake, the boys will want to eat once we get the wagon unloaded."

Cora bit her lip. Her heart cried tears, but she refused to allow her eyes to respond. Nothing had changed. She was still the woman who cared for his house, cooked his meals and watched after his child. Nothing more.

"Yes, Ramsey, I'll get to it right away."

8

Cora awoke to the clatter of the wagon rumbling around the side of the cabin. She got out of bed, pushed back the curtain and looked out the sleeping room window. She saw the rear portion of the wagon. Protruding out were pieces of lumber—lots of lumber. She hurriedly tied her wrapper around her waist and padded barefoot to the kitchen. *What was Ramsey about?*

She set the coffee pot on top the cook stove, lit the kindling inside to get a fire going. The men would be in soon for breakfast, and she'd slept late. That was getting to be a habit. She found herself tired most of the time, a result of her ever-increasing girth, and the inability to find a comfortable position in the bed.

Once the fire was ablaze, she rushed back into the sleeping area, pulled the curtain and dressed in her new blue skirt and one of Ramsey's chambray shirts. She'd decided her too-tight blouse wasn't appropriate to wear in the company of strangers. She didn't think Ramsey would mind her borrowing the garment, and if he did it'd be too late to protest by the time he saw her wearing it.

The biscuits were just coming out of the oven when the men walked into the house. "Breakfast is ready, have a seat," Cora announced.

"Sure does smell good, Miss Cora." Rusty took off his hat and tossed it to the floor, pulled out a chair and sat.

Cora placed coffee mugs on the table, dizzied for a moment by Ramsey's earthy scent as she passed his chair. Fresh rain and saddle soap. She doubled a dish towel and plucked the coffee pot off the stove. Making the rounds, she filled each cup. She fixed a cup for Treasure, adding water to weaken it.

"What's that you've got in the wagon, Ramsey?" She asked, passing the bowl of gravy.

"It's a surprise for Treasure."

"A surprise for me, Papa? What is it?"

"Well, I was thinking, you might just grow crooked if you keep sleeping curled up on the floor as you have."

"I'd givin' a bit of thought to that myself," Treasure said.

"We can't have that happen, can we?" Ramsey ruffled his son's hair. "How would you like to have your own sleeping room and bunk beds?"

"You mean it, Papa? A room to myself and a real bed to sleep in?" Treasure squished up his nose, his brow wrinkled. "What is a bunk bed? I don't think I ever heard of nothin' like that."

"It's one bed, with another built on top of it, with room in between. You'd need to climb a ladder to get to the top bed."

Ramsey grinned at Cora. "Figured this way if Henry wanted to come spend the night sometime, Treasure would have room for him to sleep over."

"Ramsey, that's an excellent idea. Are you going to add an extra room to the cabin?"

"Can I get some more of those fried taters?" Shorty interrupted. "They's sure tasty."

"Yes, of course, help yourself." Cora slid the platter toward him.

"Rusty and Shorty have some building experience, and we figured the three of us could have the add-on done in a week's time, maybe less." Ramsey looked at Cora. "Gonna be a bit of a mess in here while the work's going on. Hope you can put up with it."

"I'm sure I'll find a way to endure." Her smile didn't reveal the excitement that fluttered her heart and bounced like a ball in her chest. Ramsey was turning this small cabin into a real home. *Now, if they only had a real marriage, it would be a perfect world.*

A growing boy needs his space, and it would make where she slept a tad more private—if ever that would be of importance. Her cheeks flushed with the thought of Ramsey crawling beneath the covers. The same covers she was under.

Ramsey sopped a biscuit in gravy and plopped it into his mouth, washed it down with coffee. "I was planning to cut a doorway right where that window is." He pointed to the window on the back wall of the room. "Hate to mess it up, now you've got new curtains hung on it."

"You can reuse the window. Treasure will need light coming into his new room, so it won't be a loss," Cora suggested.

"That's what I was thinking." Ramsey raised his eyes to meet hers, grinned. "Great thoughts meeting."

"We do agree on most things, I've noticed." Cora found living with Ramsey easy to do. He was considerate of her and his son, and likewise, she wanted to please him as well. Ramsey gazed up at her. "Yes, we do. That'd be a good thing, you reckon?"

"I'd say it's perfect." Cora met his gaze, held it a moment. They were married, and yet they were strangers in the real sense. Ramsey still slept in the barn, but one day perhaps that would change. If she had anything to do with the transition, it would happen sooner than later. The words she wanted to say remained unspoken.

As soon as breakfast concluded, the men began work, carefully marking where the opening in the wall would go. It wouldn't be cut through until the new room was framed in and covered with a plank on the outside, preventing unwanted varmints from coming in during the night.

After five long work days, Treasure's new room was complete except for the beds. Ramsey spent the day cutting the doorway from the cabin into the new area, then he framed the beds and nailed them into place on the east wall. He used sturdy pieces of lumber to brace the upper bunk so that it could hold a sizable amount of weight.

Ramsey had thought of everything. He'd purchased fabric for Cora to sew into large double-sided rectangles. These bags were stuffed with straw, and then cotton batting layered on top to form a soft, not pokey, mattress to sleep. When the bed frames were complete, the mattresses were placed. With winter coming, the room made a grand space for Treasure to spend time.

"Come take a look, son," Ramsey called from the porch to the young man who'd been banished to the corral with Sara to keep him from underfoot.

Treasure came running inside and plopped down on the lower bed. "This is as soft as a cloud," he said.

"You ever had the occasion to sit on a cloud, son?" Ramsey asked.

"No sir, but I reckoned it couldn't be no better than this."

Cora stood at the door. The interaction between father and son warmed her, like cocoa on a snowy day.

"I'm thinkin', Papa, I might be needin' me a nap right about now."

"Treasure Locke, you haven't taken naps since you were three years old," Cora reminded.

"Yes'um, but I'm thinkin' I might be needin' to take one today."

Ramsey turned to Cora. "That might be a good idea. It'll keep him out of my way while I get the other project done."

They left Treasure making snow angels on his new bed and walked back into the main room. "What other project, Ramsey? Surely you aren't going to build another room?"

"I got a deal on the lumber from old Mr. Simpson at the mill. He had some pieces that'd been sitting around for a while. They were a might warped, but still usable."

"And...?"

Ramsey put his hands on Cora's shoulders. I thought it might be nice to close off your sleeping room, make it private. After the baby's here, you can put him...or her down on the bed for a nap, and the little one won't get woke up by people coming and going from the house.

"How thoughtful, Ramsey." Cora embraced an emotion she couldn't quite identify. Why would he be concerned about the well-being of her baby's sleep? It wasn't his child after all.

"If there's enough wood left once we're done, I'll tear out the wood bin on that far wall and build one at the side of the porch. That'll make space for a rocking chair so you can sit and rock the little one when you need to nurse."

Cora was taken aback. All these ideas to make the house more convenient for a new baby. "The plan is lovely, but I don't have a rocking chair. It won't be necessary to tear out the wood storage."

Ramsey's gray eyes danced. "Oh, you've got one. It's out in the barn for the time being until we get the space to bring it into the house."

"You bought a rocking chair? Why would you do that?"

He took his hat off the table and pushed it on his head, heading for the door. "Every baby needs held and rocked by its momma. It's the right thing. Your young'un should be no different." He walked out without another word.

Cora's elation fell about her feet. *Yes, my child, not yours, Ramsey. Is this the division between us?* She sighed and rubbed her swollen belly. She'd loved William with all her heart, but he was gone and would never know of this baby she carried. It saddened her, but what saddened her more was that she didn't grow Ramsey's seed.

In two days' time, the sleeping area was enclosed that housed the bed where Cora slept; the wood bin relocated to the outside of the house next to the porch. A beautiful, wooden rocking chair with roses carved on the back and arms, was placed in the sitting area ready for rocking her baby when it arrived.

Cora saw a softer side of Ramsey during those days of construction. She remembered the intensity of the kiss they'd shared, and wondered if that prompted his concern for her comfort. Neither of them had spoken of the incident, and Ramsey went through each day acting as if nothing happened, but something had. Cora found her heart open to loving a man she barely knew. Not that she'd stopped loving William. That love would always have a place in her heart, but he was gone, and she was very much alive, as was Ramsey Keaton Locke.

Alone in the house, Cora sat in the rocker and imagined how it would be to hold her baby in her arms. Would it be a boy or a girl? How would Ramsey react to the child once it arrived? He would treat it kindly, of that Cora was sure, but could he ever love the child? Could he ever love her? Somehow she didn't think his generous heart was large enough to take in them both. Still, she hoped.

After supper that evening, Ramsey announced that another set of bunk beds were constructed in the tack room out in the barn, and Rusty and Shorty would use those for as long as they stayed on at the ranch. "I'll be sleeping on the top bunk in Treasure's room."

In that instant, Ramsey got hit with the fact he hadn't given this concept near enough thought. He'd be sleeping under the same roof as the woman who'd set him afire with her kiss. Nothing but a door to separate them. He hoped he'd have the willpower to keep from knocking that door off its hinges, jumping into her bed, and making love to her until dawn. He figured he'd have a few sleepless nights trying to hold the thought of it at bay. If only she'd give him one encouraging sign, she was his wife after all, but she offered nothing of the sort. He didn't expect she ever would.

"I made a gooseberry pie. Would anyone like a piece?"

Cora's comment scattered his thoughts. Probably best. No sense making himself crazy wanting something he couldn't have. She grew large with William's baby, and he figured that was sacred territory. A boundary Cora would protect at all cost.

Shorty and Rusty stammered over each other with their, "Yes 'um" and "you betcha."

"I'll take two slices, Momma." Treasure rubbed his belly.

"Pie would taste mighty good, Cora. Thank you for making our meal special tonight." Ramsey cleared his throat. "Probably be the best meal we'll get for a long spell."

Cora stopped short, knife poised. "What do you mean? I'll continue to cook for you as I always have, and I'll only be down a couple of days when the baby comes. I'll see you don't starve, Ramsey."

"I've got no complaints about your cooking, Cora, but I won't be getting any of it for a while starting the day after tomorrow."

She wilted against the kitchen counter, her face pale and fearful. "What do you mean? What's going on?"

"Uh, Ramsey," Rusty said. "Me and Shorty will take our pie and eat it on the porch, so you and the missus can talk." The men picked up their plates and scurried out.

Cora dished pie for Treasure into a bowl. "Here, go out and keep the boys company."

Once Treasure had gone, and the door closed, Cora turned to face Ramsey, hands on her hips. "Well?"

"You don't need to fret, Cora, this is a good thing." Ramsey got up and stood beside her at the counter. "When Rusty was in Green Patch he heard talk of the cavalry wanting to buy up wild mustangs. He's got a cousin works at the railhead in Abilene, Kansas, so he checked it with him. There'll be a military representative waiting the first of next month. For every wild horse brought in, he'll pay four dollars and fifty cents."

"Over four dollars?"

"Yes, did you ever hear of such a thing? They guarantee it. I've seen a rough string running the upper Washoo ridge, close to a hundred mustangs. I figure we can rope the stallion and lead him into to the corral. The mares will follow."

"Isn't it always that way?" Cora chuckled softly.

"What?" Ramsey's brows arched.

"Never mind. Go ahead, you said you think the three of you can bring the horses down to low land?"

"If we can get control of the stallion, it won't be a problem. We hope to get them run into the corral by the day after tomorrow if we find 'em where I last saw them grazing."

"But won't wild horses try to break out?"

"We'll have to take turns standing watch through the night, keep the stallion calm."

"And then what?" Cora knew she wasn't going to like the answer that was coming.

"We'll rest up a day, leave the next morning and start for Abilene. Shorty's got a younger brother, Calvin, who

wants to go along, just for the experience, and we won't
have to split any of the pay with him. Whatever we get
from selling the horses to the cavalry, I'll share equally
with Rusty and Shorty."

Ramsey squeezed her shoulders. "I don't fancy leaving you and the boy here alone for that long, but Cora,
this would be enough money for us to get through the
winter with no worries and have seeds to plant in the
spring. We can even pick up several more head of young
breed heifers to add to what we've already got."

He took a deep breath, bent eye level with Cora.
"Come next spring several of us ranchers plan to drive
our cattle to Kansas City and sell them at the stockyards
there. That'll put the Lost C in the good, Cora." He
traced the rise of her cheek with his finger. "If we can
deliver prime stock, our brand will be in demand for future sales. It can give us a life of plenty."

"This all seems so far away for me to grasp, Ramsey."
Cora's head spun with all the possibilities. She tried to
piece together what he envisioned. One thing was sure,
if this is what Ramsey decided to do, she'd support him.

"Treasure and I will be all right. If we have a need,
the Hollisters are just a few miles down the road. Do what
you feel you must. The baby isn't due for several months
yet, so you have nothing to regret by leaving now." She ladled a cup of water and drank. Did she remember right?
When he explained his reasoning, he'd said *we* this, and
we that? Yes, she was sure he had.

He bent down and kissed the side of her mouth. She wanted to turn, allow him to take her lips fully. Instead, the kiss was brief, over before it became a reality.

"Keep a lantern lit on the table, but don't wait up. I reckon the boys and I will be up half the night finalizing details. I'll just sneak in, climb into the empty bunk in Treasure's room when we're done talking."

"As you wish, Ramsey."

He touched the tip of her nose with his knuckle, the corners of his mouth reached for his eyes. "You know, as wives go, you aren't half bad."

He turned, walked out of the house, and didn't look back.

Her heart pounded in her chest, breaking into pieces like hammered glass. She stood at the counter, inhaled Ramsey's lingering essence. His sensual scent dazzled her. Debilitated her. Damned her.

Oh, Ramsey, let me show you what a good wife I can be...give me one sign and I am yours.

9

The sun had yet to rise when breakfast was on the table. Ramsey ambled from Treasure's room to the kitchen. "The kid is trying to get his eyes open," he told Cora. "He'll be along."

"I'm sure the smell of biscuits and gravy will pull him to the table." Cora placed a platter of scrambled eggs.

Ramsey noticed the flush of Cora's cheeks from standing over a hot stove. "I sure never expected this, Cora," he said waving his hand toward the food-laden table.

"I figured you and the men needed a hardy meal to give you strength to wrangle wild horses."

The door swung open, and Rusty, Shorty, and Calvin shuffled into the room, pulled out chairs and sat. They filled their plates and ate quickly. After second helpings they rushed out to the barn to saddle the horses. Ramsey sipped coffee and watched Cora prepare a sack of biscuits and jerk meat for them to take on the trail.

"This will hold you over until you get back," Cora handed Ramsey the bag. "I'll have beans, fried potatoes and cornbread waiting on you when you return in three days' time."

"It might be late in the evening, especially if the wild string moved to another area. You and Treasure don't wait on us to eat or to bed down. Keep the beans on the stove and me and the boys will serve ourselves when we get in."

"Papa, you leavin' to go fetch them mustangs?" Treasure rubbed sleep from his eyes.

"I am, son."

"I reckon I could sure be a help to ya if'n you'd take me along."

Ramsey leaned over his plate eye level with the child. "No doubt on that score, son, but you know what'd be a real help and a worry off my mind?"

"What, Papa?"

He put a hand on the boy's arm. "I've been fretful about leaving your momma, in her condition. Then I thought, what do I have to worry about, you'd be here. I figured you could see to the chores, be sure your momma didn't overdo herself. Make certain she comes in out of the sun and rests if she gets tired. It'd be your responsibility to look after the mules, the hens and gather the eggs. Oh, and you'd have to give the team horses oats at night. Think you can man up to all that?"

"Yes sir, I can do them things. Won't take me but a spell to get it all done, so you don't be a-worryin' none."

"Now that's a relief to know." Ramsey stood and patted his son's shoulder. "Better be getting some of Cora's gravy on your plate before it's too cold to eat."

The boy straightened in his chair, split a biscuit and spooned pork gravy over it, momentarily lost in his own world.

Cora walked Ramsey to the door. "You boys keep on the slow-down out there."

"We'll take every precaution to keep the horses and us safe." He rested his forearm against the door frame. "Thanks for getting up so early to fix a hot meal for us before we left. I appreciate it."

"Doing my duty is all. I don't sleep all that much lately anyhow, with the baby growing and moving so much." Cora rested her hand against her protruding stomach, her jaw tightened.

"You all right?" Ramsey stepped closer.

"Yes. The baby wants to kick me to ribbons today."

Ramsey reached out toward Cora. "May I? I've never felt a baby move inside its mother before."

"Of course. Feel here." Cora guided his hand and placed it on her swollen belly. She smiled when the baby rose to meet his touch, as did Ramsey.

"That little tike is strong."

The baby pushed again against the pressure of his hand. An emotion Ramsey couldn't identify flowed through him like a river, like ragweed spreads in the spring, like lightning in a storm.

He pulled his hand away. "You sure you'll be all right while I'm gone?"

"Don't be silly. Treasure will be with me, and you'll be back soon."

"That's the plan," he told her. Then for no reason, he could think of, he wanted to kiss her, taste those pink heart-shaped lips again, have the memory of it to take with him. Warning bells in his head told him better, but right now his heart was running the show. He leaned toward her, his mouth a whisper from hers. The babe moved again, where Cora's belly pressed against his hip. At that moment he wanted her more than he could remember wanting anyone or anything. His lips brushed hers, and immediately she lowered her head and stepped away.

She fidgeted with her apron, eyes focused on her hands. "You'd best be on your way," she said. "You're burning daylight, aren't you?"

Ramsey couldn't explain why his heart ached like it'd been ripped from his chest. It wasn't like there'd ever been anything between them. Two brief kisses, that's all. One sealed their marriage, and the last when she'd fallen. It was obvious one of them regretted the incidents. Sure as hell wasn't him. It only made him want her more. So damn much more.

He grabbed his hat off the nail by the door. "Take care. We'll get back quick as we can."

"Ride safe," Cora said, as the door closed behind him, relieved he'd left before he could discern her distress.

Once she heard the men ride out, she found a chair and sat. Her back hurt, and she felt twinges of pain circling her stomach. She rubbed her hand over her swollen middle. The child within her moved, gently pushing against her navel. The church women she'd talked with said a baby gets real still before its birthing time. This baby often moved, so she couldn't be in labor. She wasn't due to deliver for three more months.

Cora had found a bruise on her hip, a result of her fall. It was an ugly shade of purple, with crimson blotches. She'd hit pretty hard, even with Ramsey partially breaking the fall. If he hadn't, she feared to think the consequence. However, she figured the jar and fright from the incident had caused her body to have these twinges.

After sitting for a few minutes, the pain in her back eased. She'd take it easy for a few days. Treasure could go out to the garden today and dig up what few root vegetables might remain and place them in the cellar for winter use. Making jam from the fall berries she'd picked perhaps would be better left for another day. She didn't think it a good idea to stand too long on her feet.

"All done, Momma." Treasure wadded his napkin and laid it next to his plate.

"Your belly full, young man? I've got a day's work planned for you."

It was mid-morning on the third day since the men had left and Cora kept looking to the southeast, hoping

Ramsey might have gotten a break and would get home early. As far as she could see, there was no dust in the air, and she didn't hear the rumble of running horses that might indicate they approached. She poured hot water from the kettle into the dishpan and began washing the breakfast dishes.

"You need to get the eggs gathered first thing this morning, Treasure."

"Can I ride Sara around in the yard first, 'fore I have to start my day?"

"Bring me your plate if you've finished eating. I guess a short ride would surely please the mule, but bring the eggs in first. Fair enough?"

"I'll get them eggs in the basket right now."

The boy raced from the house and was back inside with the basket in a shake. "Done, Momma. I'm goin' to get Sara now."

"All right, but go slow."Cora took the opportunity to sit in the rocker. She positioned the wooden trunk that housed extra blankets in front of the chair. Her instincts told her to elevate her feet. While Treasure and Sara spent time together in the yard, that's what she did.

She closed her eyes, remembered the feel of Ramsey's lips on hers for that brief moment. In his eyes burned a fire she'd never seen. A blaze she wanted to help him extinguish. The very instant he'd pressed his mouth against her lips she'd felt a searing stab in her low back. Her knees threatened to buckle. She'd pulled away from him and into the pain, tried to conceal her discomfort.

She'd sent him away, not looking at him again, hiding what she was sure he'd see in her eyes. Fear.

Cora sighed. What did it matter? He was a man long denied physical satisfaction, and Lord knows a man has his needs. That's all he wanted from her. She was here, right under his nose. He didn't have to clean up and go look to impress some pretty little thing in town. They had a marriage of convenience and Ramsey wanted to make the most of it, if he found her willing.

"Momma, Momma." Treasure banged the door open and rushed into the kitchen. "Momma, where are ya?"

"Here, son. I'm right here. What's wrong?" Cora got up from the rocker and held Treasure in her arms.

He gasped for breath. "I seen 'em up on the hill. Injuns. We need to hide under the bed."

"Indians?"

"Yes'um, there a-comin' to get us."

Cora had seen a few native folks milling around in town from time to time, but they caused no trouble. However, this wasn't town, and she couldn't take a chance.

"Treasure, go, climb out your bedroom window. Sneak around the back of the house and get into the cellar. Stay there until I come to get you, or until your father returns home. You don't leave unless one of us tells you. You understand?"

"But I promised Papa I'd look out for you."

"Listen to me, son. I don't think we're in any danger, but in case we are, someone will need to tell your father what happened...sayin' if I wasn't here. That'd have to be you, Treasure. Now you hide in the cellar like I told you. Hurry on."

Treasure did as told, and Cora climbed onto the wooden step stool and grabbed the rifle off the rack over the door. She'd heard nothing of Indian troubles in these parts, but that didn't mean they couldn't start today. She checked the chamber to be sure it held a shell. It did.

She watched out the kitchen window as the three Indians rode down the hill bareback on paint ponies, around the corral, and into the yard. Her hands shook. She held the gun tight; finger closed over the trigger.

"Locke, you in there?" One of the Indians shouted in English. "I come to do some trading."

He didn't sound threatening. It seemed he'd been here before, that he knew Ramsey. Cora set the gun to the side of the door frame where she could reach it if she needed to and cracked the door open. "Can I help you? I'm Mrs. Locke."

The elder man laughed out loud, slapped his hand against his buckskin-clad leg. "I thought that was only a rumor we'd heard...Locke taking a wife. I see it was the truth."

The man slid down from his horse and walked to the porch steps. "We mean you no harm, missus. I've been blood brothers with Ramsey a long time. We've hunted together. He's brought my people a cow to butcher when the winter provided us with no meat. I'm called Hawk Feather."

Cora opened the door further and stepped onto the porch. "Glad to make your acquaintance, Hawk Feather."

Again the native man laughed. "Locke calls me Sorry, 'cause he says I'm a sorry excuse for the throat cuttin', burnin'-at-the-stake savage the Army makes us all out to be." He grinned. "I've never been one of them."

Cora smiled too. "I reckoned the white man might have given cause for some of your people to turn that direction."

"Suppose there might be truth in that, but it doesn't give cause to kill for the sake of killing."

Cora noticed the elder Indian spoke like an educated man, while the other two, much younger men traveling with him, said nothing. Perhaps they were the elder's sons?

"How can I help you, Mr. Sorry?"

"I got these." He pulled two rabbits from a leather tote on his horse's rump. "Figured Locke might be up for trading them for some flour and vegetables if you got some stored. We sure have enjoyed the carrots from last summer."

"Carrots?"

"Yes. That's the crop we favor." He held the rabbits up for her to see. "Want to make a trade? These are fresh. Killed 'em this morning, and they've been bled."

Cora motioned for him to lay them on the porch. "I was hankering for a pot of rabbit stew. What a pleasant surprise." She pointed to the well. "Why don't you get a drink and I'll fix a bag of niceties to take with you."

"That's kind of you. I'd expect nothing less from Locke's woman."

While the men drank from the well, Cora scooped flour into a cloth bag and tied it shut, then went to the cellar to gather the carrots from the basket. She took enough to last Mr. Sorry's family several meals. Bundled and tied them together.

"Treasure, come out. The situation is pleasing."

The boy peeked out from behind a shelf. "You still got your hair, Momma?" he asked when he emerged from the darkness.

"You've heard too many stories, young man. The Indians are friends of your father's. They trade with him."

"What kinds of things did the Injuns have to trade ya?"

"Well, we are going to have rabbit stew for dinner when your father and the men return home, thanks to our Indian friends." She ushered Treasure toward the house. "Let me introduce you to them."

Cora slipped two dozen eggs into a covered basket, and she and Treasure waited on the porch until the men returned to their tethered horses.

Mr. Sorry grinned. "Who's this strapping young man?" he asked.

"This is Ramsey's son, Treasure. He wanted to make your acquaintance."

"Well, now, this comes as a surprise. Ramsey keeping secrets from me, I see. I'll have to speak with him on that score."

Cora wasn't sure how to respond but figured the truth was the best approach. "The child was a surprise to Ramsey as well, Mr. Sorry. He didn't know of his son until a few months ago when the child's mother passed on."

"Cora's my momma now," Treasure offered. "And I got a papa too."

"Looks like you're in grand stead, Papoose. Can't ask for more."

Sorry took the sack and basket from Cora. "Thank you, missus," he said. "You tell Locke he took a turn onto the red road in his choice of a wife. Tell him when his son is born, to send word. My village will want to bring an honoring gift, send prayers to the Great Spirit." The men jumped astride their horses as if the distance from the ground to the animal's back were mere inches.

"And what if the baby is born a girl?" Cora asked. "Will she be honored?"

"We shall ask the Great Spirit to give her a kind heart like her mother's and bring her beads for adornment. You tell Locke Sorry said these things."

"Yes, I surely will. You come back anytime, Mr. Sorry. We're happy for you to visit."

He nodded. When I return next, I'll bring warrior feathers for Treasure. He too will be a blood brother to our tribe." The elder kneed his horse's side, and the three rode down the road and out of sight. Cora wondered why Ramsey never mentioned this friend? Perhaps it'd never come to mind. It appeared it was long measures of time between visits. No matter, the unexpected event was pleasant. She was grateful.

The visit had been a distraction, but there was work to get done. "Treasure, how about you get a drink from the dipper and a leftover biscuit. That'll give you strength to clean the stalls in the barn and fork fresh straw. That's the chore I have planned for you today. Are you up to it?"

"Yes'um. I can do ever'thing you need done while Papa's away. I'm almost a grown man."

"That you are, and I'm lucky you're here."

Cora worried herself into a dither over the next two days. The men had not returned at the time predicted, and she had a chill she couldn't shake.

It was dusk on the fifth day when Cora heard the sound of horse's hooves coming from the east down the hill. "Treasure, your fat...." She turned to see the boy had fallen asleep at the table, his wooden toy horse in his hand.

She hurried to the porch to wait for Ramsey and the men to appear from the waning light into full view. *They'll want the corral gate open.* She rushed to do that and get back to the porch, out of the way.

She saw Rusty first, with the lead stallion tethered by a rope around its neck. He saw the corral open and yelled, "Yee-haw," as he rode in through the gate with the big black stallion in tow. The mares followed, with Shorty riding line to keep them going the right direction.

Where's Ramsey? I don't see him. It seemed a chaotic frenzy until all the horses were in the enclosure and the gate shut tight.

"Hobble the black," Rusty told the other man. "I'll go help bring in the boss."

Cora ran to the corral. *Something is wrong. Ramsey should be here. He isn't.* "Shorty, where's Ramsey? Why isn't he with you?"

Before he could answer, she saw Rusty meet up with two men, riding slow, silhouetted by the setting sun. She ran to the edge of the yard. Rusty took the reins of the Appaloosa, Ramsey slumped over in the saddle. Young Calvin held him steady, to keep him from falling to the ground.

"What happened?" she screamed. She saw Ramsey's blood-soaked shirt. A bandage made from a dusty bandana wrapped around his upper arm. Even in the faint light of evening, she could see the open raw flesh on his shoulder. His face was pale and drawn, eyes closed.

Rusty halted the horses, jumped down and pulled Ramsey from the saddle onto his shoulder and toted him to the house. "Where you want him, Miss Cora?"

"Put him in my sleeping room, in the big bed." She pushed the door open for him to get inside. He laid Ramsey on the bed. "Mountain lion got him."

Cora rushed to the side of the bed and felt Ramsey's forehead. "He's burning up with fever."

"We got him back as quick as we could, but he wouldn't let us leave the horses. He didn't want us losin' any more of 'em." Rusty took off his hat and rubbed the back of his neck.

"Sure am sorry about this, ma'am. It don't look too good for the boss. He should've had that wound tended a few days back."

On close examination, Cora saw the injury was not recent. The chance that infection had already set in was more than probable. The men had done the best they could, but the injury hadn't been cleaned or treated. Ramsey could die.

"Get on your horse, Rusty, get the doctor. Go as fast as you can. Time isn't on our side."

10

"*I*s Papa goin' to heaven like my other momma?" Cora turned her attention from Ramsey. Treasure stood in the doorway, his face tear-stained. "No honey, your papa isn't going anywhere but right here in bed."

"But he ain't movin'. His eyes is closed." The boy's bottom lip trembled.

"Come here, Treasure, see for yourself. He's sleeping, that's all." Cora motioned for the child to come to her side. She continued to bathe Ramsey's forehead with a damp cloth. "Your papa hurt his arm, and the pain is making him drift, but we're gonna fix him up good as new."

Treasure leaned against Cora's side, and she hugged him. "You want to help?"

"Yes'um, I'd sure like to."

"Slip on your jacket, run outside and find Shorty. I believe he's over by the corral. Tell him as soon as he can, come talk to me. Can you do that?"

"Yes'um." Treasure smiled, his shoulders squared with importance. "I'll get him right now."

It seemed long minutes before Shorty and Treasure came into the house, and all the time Ramsey made no sound. His body shook uncontrollably with bouts of chills. His breath was shallow, color ashen. Cora so much wanted to believe what she'd told Treasure, but watching her husband so still, she couldn't push away the doubt that crept into her mind.

"Miss Cora, how's he doin'?" Shorty, somber, held his hat in his hand like he was at a wake.

"Do you have the horses secured?" Cora asked.

"Hobbled the stallion. As long as he's not on the trot, the mares will stay put."

"Then there's something I need you to do."

"What is it, ma'am?" Shorty walked closer.

"Take the lantern. Go down to the creek and gather some plants."

She turned to Treasure. "Do you remember the vine I showed you a few weeks ago, the one that grows low on the ground near that old dead stump?"

"That'un with little red berries on it, Momma?"

"That's exactly the one." She took a cover from one of the pillows. "Take this and gather a bunch of the plant. Show Shorty which one I need."

Treasure took the pillowcase. "I know the way, Momma."

"Shorty, pull the vine, so it's intact. I need the whole thing, leaves, berries, and roots. You understand?"

"Yes, ma'am. I'll get right to it." He took Treasure's hand. "Show me where to go, young'un, let's be quick as a fox."

They left with the lantern to complete the task. Cora removed Ramsey's shirt and cleaned around the three deep gashes as best she could. There was reddening in the wound and pus pockets in the deepest gash, and it smelled. She hoped the plant remedy would slow the infection until the doctor arrived and did something better.

In a few moments she heard the cabin door open, and Treasure rushed in yelling, "Momma, we got it."

Shorty held up the bulging pillowcase. "What is this stuff, ma'am?"

"Birdburr. Take it to the kitchen. I'll be right there." She pulled the blanket over Ramsey's shoulders and laid the damp cloth on his forehead.

"Pour everything out on the table," Cora told Shorty, then she sorted through the vines.

Shorty set the lantern to help see better. "What ya got planned to do with this, Miss Cora?"

"Yeah, Momma, whatcha makin'?"

Cora pulled the leaves off the plant. When she had a pile, she took a knife and chopped them finely. "One of the working girls back in Kansas was a gypsy. Her grandmother was a Wise Woman among her people, and this is one of her medicines." Cora put the chopped leaves in a pan on the cook stove and added a small amount of water. "I've seen this work more than once to keep infection from setting in after some fool man jumped into a bar fight and got himself cut up with a broken bottle."

"We picked all there was, Miss Cora, least what we could find by lantern light," Shorty told her.

"Let's hope it's enough."

While the leaves steeped on the stove, Cora cut the roots off the end of the plant and picked the few berries that were left. She put those items in another pot and covered them completely with water adding several inches.

"Shorty go watch over Ramsey while I finish here. Bathe his forehead and face often with cool water from the bowl on the nightstand."

"Yes, ma'am."

"Treasure, you need to get back in your bed. Try to sleep."

"But, Momma, do I have to? I want to stay up with you and Shorty."

Cora stooped and held Treasure's hands. "I need you to be wide awake tomorrow, son. I'll need someone who can look over your papa while I'm cooking the meals. Shorty, Rusty and Calvin will be busy with the horses." She ruffled his hair. "Can't have you falling asleep when you're on watch duty, can we?"

"No, ma'am. I see your reasonin'. Goodnight, Momma."

"Sleep tight, son."

In the kitchen, Cora spooned the limp leaves from the pot and placed them in a sieve to drain. Then she wrapped them in a dishtowel, twisted it tight to wring out the remaining liquid. She took the moist concoction and went to the bedroom where Ramsey lay and relieved Shorty from his vigil.

Shorty stood by the door. "If you ain't gonna need me for nothin' more, Miss Cora, I'll go bed down myself. Lots to get done tomorrow."

"Thank you for your help, Shorty. I'll be fiddle now. Goodnight."

"Yes'um."

Sitting on the bed next to Ramsey, she pressed the leaves into the gashes made by the mountain lion's claws then bound his arm with a clean cloth. He felt cooler to the touch, and that was a good sign. She pulled the blanket over his chest. He moaned softly, mumbling, incoherent. "Lay still, Ramsey. Doc Olson's on his way."

Back in the kitchen, Cora poured the broth from the roots and berries into a cup. She took a spoon from the drawer and returned to her patient. "Ramsey, can you sip a little of this?" She held a spoonful of juice to his lips, parting them slightly with the tip of the spoon. He lapped at the liquid with his tongue but most dribbled down his chin. She tried again. This time he took more. After she'd gotten a good portion of the brew into him, she set the cup aside, pulled a chair next to the bed and sat.

Sun streaming through the window woke Cora. She blinked sleep from her eyes and immediately put her hand to Ramsey's head. He was hot again, but not as bad as when the men had brought him home. She went to get a fresh bowl of cool water to wash him.

"Ho. Ho team," someone yelled as a wagon rumbled into the yard.

Please, let that be the doctor. Cora rushed to the door "Thank God, you're here." She waved Doc Olson inside.

"Sorry, I couldn't come sooner, Cora. I was delivering the Johnson baby, and it took a might longer than thought."

"You're here now. That's all that matters. Come. Hurry."

Cora explained to Doc what had happened and that the wound had gone unattended for nearly two days. "I cleaned it best I could, but some infection has set in."

The doctor removed the bandage and looked. "These cuts are quite deep. What's this green poultice you have on it?"

"Birdburr vine, it grows down by the creek." She explained how she'd come to know of it. "I've seen it work before on cut up cowboys after a bar brawl, and I had to try something until you could come. I made a tea from the berries and roots and have given him some of that too."

"I'd say it's done a good job." Doc probed the damaged arm, pulling the flesh this way and that. "There's still infection, but it's not too red." Doc leaned over, stuck his nose near the wound and sniffed. "No foul or-der, that's a real indication there's healin' goin' on and not more deterioration of tissue."

"That's good, right?"

"It's certainly is. However, we need to take some stitches and close up the gashes so it can heal properly. Doc pulled a spool of catgut from his bag and a needle. "I don't think he'll feel anything, but if he does, we'll stop and give him a bit of chloroform.

All in all, Doc took twenty-two stitches in Ramsey's arm. When he'd finished, he gave instructions to Cora. "Keep puttin' that poultice you made on the injury when you wrap it with a clean cloth."

He took a bottle of pills from his bag and poured out six. "Crush one of these and put it into the tea you made and see that he drinks it all."

"What are these?" Cora took the pills from the doctor.

"Sulfur. It should help with the infection along with what you're already doin'." Doc closed his bag and stood. "Another thing, I want the bandage changed every eight hours. Put less of the poultice on the wound, but do it more often. Can you manage that?"

"Yes, I'll see to it, Doc Olson. How often do I give him a pill?"

"Twice a day. One in the morning and one after sup-pertime. Let him sleep through the night if he can. Rest is essential to his healing right now."

Cora walked with the doctor to the door. "See you day after tomorrow then."

"In the late afternoon, I 'spect."

"I'll have fresh eggs waiting for you to take home when you leave, Doc. You're welcome to take a chicken too if you'd like."

"A couple dozen eggs is payment enough, dear lady. Thank you."

She waved the doctor off and shut the door.

Cora sat with Ramsey part of the day, and Treasure stayed by him while she chopped and steeped more of the birdburr leaves. She poured the tea into a fruit jar and stored it in the cellar to keep it palatable until she needed it. She'd managed to get the first sulfur pill into Ramsey, and hoped he'd soon be fully conscious.

Between Treasure, the two hands, Rusty and Shorty, and young Calvin all the daily chores got done. When they all sat at the kitchen table that evening eating smoked rabbit stew for supper, Shorty fidgeted.

"Something you need to say?" Cora asked.

Well, me and Rusty was wonderin' how long you think the boss is gonna be bed-rid?"

"I can't answer for sure. It will depend on when Ramsey wakes up and can talk to us. Is there a reason you're asking?"

He cleared his throat. "The Army is only gonna be at the railhead for one week, at the first of the month. If we don't get them mustangs to Abilene by then, we'll miss out on selling 'em for top dollar."

"It's early yet. You have nearly a month before you'd have to be there," Cora said.

"Yes ma'am, only thing is, it's gonna take us near to three weeks to get the string moved that far and not run 'em lean. So we don't have but a few days to spare 'fore it's too late."

She sensed the men's disappointment. "If Ramsey isn't up and able in five days, you'll need to find someone else who can ride with you, take the horses and sell to the cavalry as planned. You boys split the money between yourselves and whoever goes with you. Ramsey will understand. He'd want it no other way."

"We'll wait 'til the last minute 'fore headin' out, ma'am," Rusty confirmed.

"That's kindly of you. Now finish your supper."

Treasure was asleep, and the men bedded down in the barn. Cora heated water on the stove, stripped down, bathed and put on a fresh nightshirt. She prepared more poultice and carried it along with clean strips of cloth to change the dressing on Ramsey's arm.

The wound looked better, swelling down, and his brow was cool to the touch.

"You're getting better, Ramsey. Maybe you'll wake up tomorrow," she said. In his state, he wouldn't hear her words, but she hoped they might somehow speed his healing. "I'll bed down in the extra bunk in Treasure's room, but I'll come and check on you every few hours." She leaned over the bed and turned down the lantern.

Ramsey's arm circled her waist, rope tight. "Don't leave me, Cora. Lay with me. Comfort me through the night."

"Ramsey...I..."

"Please."

In the darkness, she couldn't see his face if his eyes were open or closed. All she knew was his touch warmed her, like the sun on a frosty day. She liked it. She pulled her feet up and slid them under the cover, spooning her back to his hard, bare stomach. "As you wish, Ramsey."

He drew her close. His manhood hardened, pressed against her juncture.

Cora's breath caught. A flame of desire she'd never experienced rushed her senses. She froze, unable to move, to protest.

Truth be told, she didn't want to.

11

Cora bit down hard on her lower lip. *Is he going to take me...like this?* She lay paralyzed, her woman place moist and aflame. Her body begged to push against his hardness, to open to him. *What is happening?* She was a woman expecting a child. *You don't have relations with a man during this time. Do you?*

Her fears faded with Ramsey's soft snoring. He wilted, went limp. She should get up, retreat to the bed in Treasure's room, but his injured arm rested possessively across her waist. Warm and relaxed, her eyelids grew heavy. Exhaustion from worry and the daily care Ramsey required took control. What she wanted most was a few moments of uninterrupted sleep. She was comfortable lying next to him, felt secure and protected. With that thought, she drifted into deep slumber.

The rooster's crow indicated a new day, even though the sun had not risen in the sky. Cora, half asleep, snuggled into the covers, savoring one more brief moment before she'd need to get up, start the coffee brewing and get breakfast in the pan.

It was when she realized Ramsey's hand had found its way between the buttons of her nightshirt and cupped one breast that she came fully awake. Her nipple hardened against his palm. The warmth of his touch brought with it desire.

During the night he'd swung his leg over her hip, and her gown gathered about her waist, leaving her bare below. Ramsey stirred, gently squeezed her breast, rubbed his thumb over the swollen peak. Again, she felt him grow hard, but this time his manhood was raw against her, pushing to gain entry.

Oh, mercy. I can't allow it. There was no denying this closeness between them created desires that exploded for fulfillment.

They weren't husband and wife in a real sense. To allow the moment to consume them would be a false reality. An act of passion they'd regret later. Well, Ramsey would. Cora chose not to linger on that thought.

Ramsey, groggy from sleep and chaotic dreams, was nonetheless aware his body reacted to the warm flesh that lay beside him. He ached like he'd been dragged, foot caught in the stirrup, behind a rattlesnake-scared gelding. Yet, his desire to couple with the woman in his bed was potent. Undeniable.

He felt her nipple grow taut against his fingers and it made him harder, desperate to push himself into her warm, wet sweet spot. He needed her, wanted her, had to take the opportunity to show her he was her husband in every way.

Ramsey prodded, gently, until he found the opening he searched for, swollen and ready. He positioned his leg between hers, lifted enough for him to enter. Slow at first, pushing in. Sliding out. In. Out. In. Out.

It didn't take long before he reached the point of no return. It'd been a very long time since he'd made love to a woman and his release barreled fast. He wanted to stay himself until she caught up, but he wasn't sure he could. *Slow down—slow down.*

Cora trembled, the first sign that she neared the same release he held back. He thrust fast and hard, and she softly cried out his name, her woman muscles squeezed him tight. In. Out. In. Out. "Oh...ahhh." He shot into her—hot and plenty.

The exertion caused his mind to go fuzzy; inky blackness came to claim him again. His last thought was of Caroline. He'd given her five years of mourning. It was time to begin a new life. "Caroline, I'm sorry."

Darkness overtook him.

Cora was jolted into her body, into the bed she shared with Ramsey. His words rang loud in her ear. *Caroline....*

He thought he'd been with Caroline, not her. Was he apologizing, thinking he'd taken advantage of a woman he'd not married? Silent tears streaked Cora's face. The joke was on her.

When his breathing deepened, she slipped from the bed and from the embrace of the man she'd come to love. She'd hoped he might have found love for her too, but now she knew different. It was Caroline he longed to be with...she claimed his heart.

An hour later, Rusty, Shorty, and Calvin were on the porch waiting to be called in for breakfast. Cora opened the door. "Come, get coffee while I finish frying the pork meat." She rousted Treasure, told him to dress and come to the table.

Everyone ate like it was their last meal. Shorty was on his second helping when Ramsey shouted from the bedroom. "Something sure smells good, reckon I could get some?"

They all rushed to find him sitting up in the bed, a smile on his face.

"Boss, you're among the livin'. Glad to see it." Rusty shoved the piece of salt pork he held into his mouth.

"Yeah, we sure didn't know if we'd get you on the mend or not," Shorty said.

"Glad to see ya better, Mr. Locke." Calvin waved.

Ramsey lifted up the covers and glanced beneath. "If I could get someone to find my drawers and a shirt, I'd like to come and share the table this morning."

Cora felt her cheeks blaze with the memory of Ramsey naked beneath the blanket. If anyone noticed she hoped they'd think she was red from standing over the stove all morning.

"You're not leaving that bed, mister," she said, ushering the men out. "Treasure, you sit here by your father and make sure he doesn't put a foot on the floor." She eyed Ramsey with a look that would knock most men unconscious. "I'll fix a plate and bring it to you."

"Coffee, too...please," Ramsey called after her.

"Of course."

When he'd finished eating, Cora changed the bandage on his arm. He watched her hands. "You do that pretty well," he said. "You're good at a lot of things, I reckon." He smiled.

"It's good you've noticed." She didn't indicate that she read anything into his words. "You stay put. I've got chores to be done. I'll check on you when I've finished."

"Cora, I gotta get up, gain my strength so we can get those horses moved to Abilene. We're gonna be short as it is."

"The boys said if they leave here by the day after tomorrow they can make it to the railhead before the buyer leaves. Rusty, Shorty, and young Calvin will take them. They'll get someone else to ride drag if Doc says you're not able to make the trip."

"Not able, hell." Ramsey sat upright. "Did you forget I'm a doctor, also? I should know if I'm fit or not. I'm going, and you best get any other thoughts out of your pretty little head, Miss Sutton."

"It's Mrs. Locke, actually." So, he didn't even consider her his *Missus* even though she carried his name. "It's been discussed, Ramsey, and agreed on. Doc says you could lose your arm if you don't heal properly. So if you're not fit to ride, the boys will solicit help and take the mustangs to Abilene. They've agreed you'll have a finder's fee of ten percent and the remainder of the money split between the riders. That seems fair."

"I'm not arguing it's not fair. I'm just saying I'm going. We lost about half-dozen mares, did the boys tell you that?"

"They mentioned you wouldn't let them leave the trail to get you home sooner because you didn't want to lose more stock." Cora poured warm herbal tea into a glass. "Drink this."

Ramsey took a swig of the liquid, wrinkled his nose and puckered his lips. "What are you trying to do, kill me?"

"Learn to love it. It's what's saved you to this point." She stood stiffly at the end of the bed. "How did you lose the horses?" she offered concern.

"When that mountain lion took after me, there was chaos for a bit. It was all Shorty could do to keep the stallion from breaking free. Several of the mares scattered and the lion took chase. He got one, but the others ran into the hills. There was no way with me bleeding like a slaughtered goat we could give chase, so we took what was left and headed for home." He downed the rest of the bitter tea and washed the taste out of his mouth with cold coffee. "We're gonna be short about seventy-five dollars on what we figured to split. We need that money, Cora, to get us through the winter, so I've got to be one of the men who takes them north."

"Doc Olson will be here sometime tomorrow to check on your wound. We'll see what he says then." Cora turned to leave the room. "I'll be about the morning chores, Ramsey. I'll leave Treasure sitting on the porch. If you need anything, give a shout."

"I'm going, Cora. You can take that to the bank," he yelled after her.

"We'll see."

Ramsey heard the front door slam shut. Cora acted somewhat stand-offish considering what had happened between them in the early hours of the morning. Maybe she was embarrassed, it being their first time together and all, and the way it'd happened. Most women he'd found, except those who worked as professionals, thought there was only one way a man could enter a woman—her on her back staring at the ceiling. Hell, he hadn't even kissed her or caressed her. Well, he only had one arm of much use at the moment. That should cut him some slack in the matter.

He felt drained all of a sudden. Maybe Cora was right, and he wouldn't be fit to ride with the boys. He'd sleep now. If he could get a good day's rest, surely by tomorrow, he'd be ready to leave the bed.

Cora finished gathering the eggs, put oats out for the team horses and filled the water troughs. Shorty said he'd ride up to check on the cattle grazing in the west pasture. They needed to keep them fat so they'd bring a decent price in the spring after calving.

She checked on Ramsey when she got back into the house and found him sleeping. Good, that's what would allow him to heal. Closing the bedroom door to keep the noise out, she called to Treasure.

"How about you gather some dandelion greens from the other side of the barn. You know where I mean?"

"Yes'um. You gonna cook some up with pork grease?"

"I thought I might do that very thing. How does that sound for supper today, with some fresh fried eggs to go with it?"

The boy rubbed his belly. "Sure would be pleasin' to my stomach, Momma. Reckon our visitors would like chowin' down on that too."

Cora turned to face the counter, hiding a smile. "Then you best get to it, son."

"Yes 'um," he said, running out the front door. A second later Treasure poked his head back inside the doorway. "Momma, I reckon I best take the straw basket with me. My arms ain't that long yet. I can carry more in the basket. I reckon Calvin's gonna want seconds, so I'd better pick plenty of them greens."

"You're a smart boy, Treasure. Did anyone ever tell you that?" Cora took the basket off the counter and handed it to him.

He grinned and took off in a run.

The day came and went without much fanfare. The wild horses seemed a bit unsettled, but Shorty kept them in tow. Ramsey slept most of the day, except when she heard him sit up on the side of the bed to use the chamber pot she'd placed for his convenience.

She tried to ignore her disappointment. He hadn't wanted to make love to her, but rather to the woman he couldn't forget. She'd never been with a man in that way before, him lying behind her. She had to admit, even in her condition she'd been more aroused than she'd thought possible, hadn't wanted it to end. When it did, she hoped it could begin again. That was before Ramsey spoke Caroline's name.

Cora kneaded the biscuit dough with fury, wishing it was her husband she was beating some sense into. She picked up the glob and slammed it against the counter, venting her frustration.

"That's gonna end up hardtack if you keep punching it like you're killing a rattler."

She turned to see Ramsey standing in the bedroom doorway, pale-skinned and raccoon around the eyes.

"Why are you out of bed?" she asked, hands on hips.

"How could a man sleep with all that pounding?"

"Sorry, I didn't mean to wake you." Cora wiped her hands on her apron.

Ramsey pulled out a chair and sat. "I was awake, lots on my mind."

He looked at her, his eyes filled with some emotion she couldn't read. It pulled like a magnet and ignited the fire in her belly again. Cora forced herself to stand rooted to her spot. She couldn't allow him to entice her into his bed again. That was a mistake she wouldn't make twice.

He glanced toward the door. "I figured if I was going to get any strength back I need to stay out of the bed a bit more. I thought I'd sit here at the table with everyone and enjoy your company for supper. How'd that be?"

"As you wish, Ramsey."

He looked at her again; his dark eyes held her gaze. He licked his lips, and a grin curled the corners of his mouth. "Would that be your answer if I asked you to come lay in my bed again, Cora?"

12

Cora wanted to scream, *not even if you built me a stairway to the stars*. Instead, she ignored Ramsey's comment. How could he think she would crawl into his bed when he'd prepared it for someone else. No, no, never.

She went to the door and opened it. "Rusty, Shorty, Calvin, get washed up for supper. Treasure, put Sara in the pen and come eat."

She left the door open although the breeze was cool. It offered her some means of escape—from what she wasn't sure. Electricity filled the air, and it wasn't because another storm brewed. Cora inhaled a guarded breath. She wouldn't give cause to emotions that served no purpose.

She placed a large bowl of greens on the table. A platter of fried eggs and a plate of biscuits finished off the meal. Treasure and the men came in as she placed the flatware.

Surprised to see Ramsey sitting at the table, Shorty and Rusty bombarded him with questions. "How ya feelin', boss? Still look a might pallid," Rusty said.

Shorty pulled out a chair. "Think you can sit a saddle, Ramsey?"

Cora bit her tongue to keep from shouting, *depends on what the doctor says when he comes to check Ramsey's wound tomorrow.* Her words would fall on deaf ears, so she held them.

"What's the latest you figure we could pull out and still make it to the railhead in Kansas in time to meet with the buyer?" Ramsey asked.

"Tomorrow'd be ideal, boss, but we know Doc's is plannin' to come check you out then. Me and Rusty have done some calculatin' and we agree if we could leave out of here day after, and make our first day's ride a long one, we'd still arrive with one maybe two days to spare. The way I got it, the Army was takin' all the mustangs they could get, but ya never know how many hands might show up with horses to sell. We don't want to get hung wantin' by gettin' thar too late." Shorty spooned a large portion of greens onto his plate. "Pass them biscuits will ya, Calvin?"

The evening continued with conversations between the men on how and when they'd move the horses to the railhead. Cora busied herself sewing some baby gowns she'd cut from a swatch of muslin purchased at the mercantile. She'd set her heart on a few yards of pretty green print. It'd make nice into another skirt, but she didn't have enough to purchase that and the muslin. The baby would need gowns, and a few blankets as well. She had seven dollars left, so she'd buy flannel to cut and hem for blankets the next time she was in town. Her child would be born in early spring, and there'd be some cold nights yet before summer made it too hot to sleep.

She'd looked at the pretty white crib the store had for sale, but that was a luxury her baby wouldn't have. The bed she slept in was big enough for her and the little one, and she'd place pillows near the edge to keep the baby from rolling off. It wasn't ideal, but it would do.

While she washed dishes, the men hovered together over coffee. She suspected they made final plans organizing the trip north. Ramsey seemed to be giving instructions to the other two. He wasn't going to pay any mind to Doc Olson if he told him he was in no shape to ride. Cora knew that in her soul. He'd go and be damn the consequences. Well, why should she care if he did some fool thing that could break open his wound, and cause more damage than had already been done? She'd noticed he'd eaten left-handed at supper, the fingers on his right hand not fully able to grasp the fork. He had muscle damage, maybe nerve damage too, yet he would be fool enough to make this journey, even against doctor's orders.

Cora put her sewing away and joined Treasure, who sat on the floor playing with his wooden horse and some sticks he'd fashioned into a corral. "Time to get ready for bed now."

"Aw, Momma, do I have to?"

"Don't argue with your mother, son. Do as she says," Ramsey ordered.

"Yes, sir." Treasure put his toys into a canvas bag and placed them on top of the dish cabinet. "Do I have to wash all over, since we still got company?" he asked.

"Your face and hands will do for tonight," Cora told him, understanding his embarrassment at stripping down at the wash basin, within sight of the hands. In his room, she helped Treasure get into his night clothes and tucked him in. "I'll be turning in soon myself. Sweet dreams, son."

"Yes'um." His sleepy hazel eyes fluttered shut as he spoke. He was asleep before Cora left the room.

Cora covered the washed dishes with a tea towel. She'd put them away in the morning.

"I think you boys need to head to the barn. Ramsey's been up long enough, and I need to get some rest myself."

"Yeah, boys, I'm feeling a bit weary, although I hate to admit it. Not bouncing back as fast as I hoped I would. Better get a good's night sleep, so I can make a fair impression on Doc when he comes tomorrow. I want him to cut me loose."

"Like it will matter if he doesn't." Cora slapped her hand against her mouth. She'd spoken out of turn. Instead of the reprimand she expected from Ramsey, he chuckled.

"She knows me well, boys." He looked in her direction. "A wife *is* supposed to know the ways of her husband, isn't that right?"

"Don't ask me, boss. I ain't never had a wife. Not lookin' neither," Rusty said.

"I'm too dang old to take a bride, too set in my ways," Shorty offered.

"I got my eye on a pretty little thing. If''n I prove myself on this here trail drive, I jest might be a askin' for her hand." Calvin grinned.

The men hee-hawed as they walked out the door to bed down in the barn.

Cora knew the implication in Ramsey's words, but she wasn't going to give credence to it. She couldn't allow the memory of their intimate moment to creep into her mind. It made her skin flush, her hands sweat, and her knees weak. She wasn't about to allow Ramsey knowledge that his touch affected her in such a way, especially when he played a game. It was Caroline he truly wished to embrace. Cora made up her mind right then and there. *I won't be a substitute for the woman who holds your heart, Ramsey.* Even if the other woman posed no present threat. Even if it was Cora's only chance to love him. Not even then.

She went to the kitchen counter and gathered several clean strips of white cloth torn for bandaging. She made a fresh batch of poultice using the last of the leaves from the birdburr plant. Cora poured the last of the berry and root tea from the jar on the counter. Luckily, there was still a pint of the tea stored in the cellar, but when it was gone there would be no more.

"Come, Ramsey, let me get your bandage changed, and get this tea down you so we can both get to bed."

Again, he smiled, the twinkle back in his eyes. "Sounds like a grand idea to me."

He got up and strolled toward the sleeping room, unbuttoning his shirt and pulling it off as he went.

Cora found herself short of breath watching the movement of his muscled back, hard and sinewy as he walked. She ran into a chair because she didn't pay attention where she was going. Her eyes held fast on Ramsey.

He turned. "You all right?"

"Fiddle. I'm perfectly fiddle."

He chuckled as he stretched his six-foot frame on the bed, legs crossed at the ankles. The two top buttons of his Levis undone. Dark hair scattered across his chest and formed an arrow straight to those buttons and below. Her eyes involuntarily followed the trail. She swallowed hard.

"See anything you'd like to touch?" Ramsey asked.

"Absolutely not," Cora croaked like a stomped frog. "Here, drink this tea. Maybe this time it *will* poison you."

"Oh, surely you wouldn't want that, would you, Cora?"

"Perhaps it will serve to cleanse your mind of vile thoughts." She jerked the bandage away from his arm, taking no pains to be careful.

"Ouch, that hurts." He pulled away. "You don't have to be mean."

"Then you best lay here and be quiet, like a little mouse in the corner, and let me finish the task at hand."

Ramsey groaned low in his throat but didn't say anything. He watched her place the green poultice on each of the stitched gashes in his arm and carefully fold the bandage material around it, making sure it was snug, but not too tight. "How can you be so kind in administering aid to my wound and yet turn a cold shoulder to sharing a bed with me?

Ramsey was looking for a door to open between them, but she'd nail the damn thing shut before she'd be a stand-in for Caroline.

"Finish off this tea." She pushed the cup sitting on the night table close enough for him to grasp. "Get yourself undressed and under the covers, please. I'll be back to get the cup and turn the lantern down in a few minutes." She gathered the old dressing and left the room quickly.

Being so near Ramsey made her head swim. His body bare on the bed tempted her resolve, convoluted her logical thinking. She wanted nothing more than to explore that tanned tight body with her hands, touch him in places she'd never laid a hand to a man before. She'd be glad when he rode out, driving the horses to Abilene, and he would, no matter what the doctor said. It would give her a few weeks to regain her composure—to forget the uncontrolled pleasure it brought to have Ramsey inside her, her body burning with the need for more of him. She must forget. It served no good. He wanted Caroline, not her. Cora didn't think there was enough love in her to change that. *I can't fight your memory of Caroline, Ramsey. Nor will I. That is a battle you must fight for yourself...if ever you have the gumption.*

Cora checked on Treasure. He slept soundly. She covered his exposed leg with the blanket and brushed a tuft of dark hair from his forehead. He was an exact copy of Ramsey, except for the color of his eyes. He'd gotten his mother's beautiful yellow-green eyes.

She slipped into her nightshirt and then into her wrapper, tied the sash tightly around her bulging belly. Barefoot she made her way to the other sleeping room to retrieve the teacup. She hoped Ramsey had downed it all so she could turn down the lantern and leave him be. Perhaps he'd drifted off to sleep by now. He'd spent much of the evening sitting at the table talking with the men, and it'd worn on him.

When she entered the room, his eyes were shut. She reached out to pick up the cup, and he grabbed her wrist.

"Stay with me tonight, Cora. Sleep in my bed."

She was thrown off balance. The mere touch of Ramsey's hand on her arm sent tingles of desire radiating through her body. She wanted to rip away her wrapper and gown, lay with him naked under the covers. She wanted his hands to roam her body until she soared. She wanted to feel him inside her, to fill her as he'd once done. Then she remembered, it wasn't her he truly desired. She jerked her arm free, stepped back.

"You'd best get your rest tonight if you have any hope of showing Doc Olson you're fit to ride a horse." She bent to turn the wick on the lantern and extinguish the flame.

Ramsey sat up, reached for her again. "I'm in need, woman. You can take care of that if you'd lay with me. We *are* married, Cora."

It took all her fortitude to turn away. She wouldn't let him see the tears, read the truth in her eyes. "You've given me your name, Ramsey Locke, a most kind gesture. Graciously I've accepted it, but we don't have a marriage. There's much more involved in creating a real marriage than what happened between us."

"What I'm proposing tonight, Cora could change that. If you'd stay with me, let me make love to you. We'd truly be husband and wife."

She mustered her strength. "No, I cannot allow it."

"Why can't you? Why have you set your mind against it...after what happened this morning?" he pleaded. "You can't stand there and tell me that didn't mean something."

"This morning was a mistake, Ramsey, something that happened while I wasn't yet awake, still in a dream state. And you, for God's sake, were barely conscious. It's a dire circumstance that shouldn't have come to pass. It wouldn't be appropriate for either of us if it occurred again. Surely, Ramsey, you can see the logic in my words?" *Besides, you weren't making love to me. You were caressing a phantom.*

Cora didn't look at him, but rushed from the room, tears streaming down her cheeks. Her heart shattered into a million jagged pieces. She'd fled from the man she loved. Left him alone. In the dark. Wanting.

13

Wearing Levi jeans and a flannel shirt, Ramsey moseyed into the kitchen, leisurely filled a cup with coffee and then bolted out the door.

"Ramsey Locke, you're not supposed to be up and about," Cora yelled, following him to the porch.

He waved his hand, kept walking fast, didn't look back and offered no comment.

"Darn fool." He'd made his mind. He was finished recuperating, and her protest wouldn't undo his thought on the matter.

Cora busied herself in the kitchen. The men kept to the barn all morning. She heard an occasional clang or clink. Were they loading the wagon? Had they decided to take it on the trail? Perhaps Rusty or Shorty convinced Ramsey he'd need to rest more and figured he could ride in the wagon while they traveled. The moment that thought popped into her head she shook it loose. There was no way Ramsey would ride in the back of a wagon while the other men rode line on horseback. Nope. Not a chance in a hailstorm.

She turned the browned biscuits onto a plate and set them on the table. Out on the porch, Cora rang the dinner bell and yelled, "Breakfast is ready."

The men came running and gathered around the table. Rusty and Shorty gobbled down eggs, salt pork and biscuits with gravy. Young Calvin was already taking seconds, and Treasure did most of the talking.

"Papa, I was wonderin' if you might have a minute to show me how to hammer a nail?

"You come out to the barn when you've finished the chores your momma has for you this morning, and I'll see if I can't find a board, and you can try your hand." Ramsey gently grabbed his son's shoulder. "After chores, not before."

"I'll get 'em done real fast then," Treasure said, with a grin.

Cora didn't sit with the men, but remained at the kitchen counter, rolling out extra biscuit dough to bake for them to take when they left for the railhead.

"You aren't eating, Cora?" Ramsey asked.

"I'll get a bite once you all finish." She didn't turn to look at him.

"Suit yourself."

The ranch hands, between bites, speculated on how soon the next day they should hit the trail. "I reckon about daylight, ya think, Ramsey?" Shorty asked.

"That'd be my thought," he agreed

"I'll have a hot breakfast to start you out in the morning," Cora stated, rinsing beans, picking out the bad ones.

"Thank ya kindly, ma'am," Rusty said. "'Preciate it."

During the day, Cora heard hammers pounding from the barn, sounding as if Ramsey gave Treasure an extensive lesson in how to set a nail. She gathered the eggs, letting her son off light on chores. It was the last day he'd spend with his father for several weeks. Ramsey looked much better today, but she didn't think he was up to the hard trip ahead. However, she knew him well enough to know that wasn't going to make a difference.

Lunch came and went, and still Doc had not arrived. Ramsey got antsy, although Cora couldn't imagine why. Whatever the doctor's opinion regarding her husband's injured arm, it wouldn't change his course of action, of that she was sure. Perhaps, Ramsey hoped Doc would give a good report so he could leave her and Treasure with some comfort in his going.

She knew Ramsey had respect for her, valued the way she cared for Treasure, was willing for her to satisfy his physical want. Even her expanded belly didn't deter him. No man would look on a woman in her condition and see beauty. She knew Ramsey's needs were what drove him.

With her girth larger each day, she labored to complete the chores while carrying the extra weight. She'd wondered if perhaps she'd miscalculated her due date, but was sure there were two months or more before she'd give birth. The baby rode high under her ribs, a sign she wasn't yet ready to deliver.

It was the middle of the afternoon when Doc Olson pulled into the yard. "Mrs. Locke, you got a bucket of water on hand? I'm parched," he yelled, climbing down from the wagon.

Cora ladled a cup and had it waiting when he got to the porch.

"Where's Ramsey, sleeping?"

Cora pointed. "He's in the barn, been there all day."

The doctor handed her the cup. "He's got no business out of the house this soon. Couldn't you keep him inside?"

"Have you ever tried to keep a bear in a chicken coop, Doc? He's headstrong on riding with the boys to Abilene and nothing you're gonna say makes a hoot."

"That a fact? Go fetch him, and I'll sit a spell 'til he gets to the house."

"Help yourself to a chair. I'll get Ramsey."

Cora headed toward the barn, but when she got halfway, Treasure came running out.

"Momma, you can't come inside. Papa don't want you to."

"Oh, you don't say?" Cora's feathers ruffled. So now the barn was off limits. Next, he'd chalk a line in the house she couldn't cross. "Then tell him Doc's here waiting on him."

"Yes'um." The boy ran back toward the barn, yelling. "Papa, you gotta go to the house, the doctor's come to see ya."

In a few minutes, Ramsey showed himself, took a chair next to Doc. "You finally made it. I was wondering if you'd fallen into a well."

"Didn't know you were in a hurry to see me, Ramsey. You plannin' on going somewhere?"

Ramsey cocked an eyebrow. "I see you've been talking to my wife."

"She tells me you got some foolhardy notion about ridin' horseback all the way to Kansas." Doc opened his medical bag and took out a pair of scissors. "Let's take a look at that arm, see how near healed it is."

Ramsey removed his arm from his shirt and waited while the doctor examined the wound. "I'm greatly surprised with this recovery, never expected it to look this good in just a few days."

Doc addressed Cora. "That poultice and tea you made up surely must be the reason for this. I've never seen anything promote a healing so fast."

"Then I'm free to go tomorrow, Doc?" Ramsey smiled and gave Cora a *told you so* look.

Doc placed his scissors back in his bag. "Ramsey, it's not my recommendation for you to take off on a ride as hard as the one you're in for. You still got stitches, and if the wound breaks open, you'll be in worse shape than when Shorty and Rusty drug you home."

"I'll be careful, Doc. I swear." *Should I say more?* "I've had a bit of medical training, Doc, so I'm aware of the danger."

Medical training. Is that a fact?" Doc Olson pursed his mouth and crossed his arms over his chest.

"Yep. However, I've found ranching more to my liking, and that means doing the job at hand."

The doctor heaved a defeated breath. "Cora, you got some of those bandages left and more berry tea?"

She picked up a stack of white, torn strips of cloth. "I can make up more if need be. I have a pint of birdburr tea sitting in the cellar. Want me to go get it?"

"Ramsey will need to take that with him when he leaves in the morning." He turned his attention back to his patient. "You promise this woman of yours that you'll drink some of that tea every night when you stop to camp." Doc shook his finger at Ramsey. "Do it."

"Yes, I promise to gulp that poison every day." He started to slide his arm into his shirt, but Doc held up a hand to halt him.

"Cora, can you put a clean bandage on the wound? Your handiwork's neater than mine."

She carried the strips to the table and laid them down. "Of course, Doc."

As she wound the material around his arm, she felt the burn of Ramsey's eyes. "That's only one of the things you do well, woman."

Her face heated at his innuendo. Luckily it went unnoticed by the doctor.

"All finished." She picked up the discarded bandages. "I need to call Treasure inside. It's his quiet time." Cora tossed the dirty dressing into the trash bin and hurried outside.

"Here's the plan, Ramsey," Doc began. "You have Rusty or Shorty wash up real good when you camp, one of 'em needs to change this dressing every day. You'll be pickin' up all sorts of dirt and grime on the trail, and if you don't have something clean covering your wound, those particles will go right into it. You understand the importance of what I'm tellin' you?"

"Yes, sir, I do. I'll make sure it's done." A chuckle caught in Ramsey's throat. He was a physician; he knew the protocol. Of course, no one in Rabbit Glen was aware of his past profession, although seeing the gleam in Doc Olson's eyes, Ramsey thought perhaps he had a good idea.

"Then, I'll take my leave. Good luck getting' those wild horses down the trail."

Ramsey stood and walked with Doc to the door. "Thanks. We're gonna need it."

Doc set his hat on his head and stepped off the porch. "Oh, one other thing, Ramsey. Those stitches need to come out long before you'll be back here. See if you can find a doctor that'll do that for ya when you arrive at your destination."

"Sure thing, Doc. I happen to know a couple of physicians that have their practices near Abilene. I'll contact one as soon as we get the horses corralled."

"Goodbye, Doc Olson," Treasure hollered as Cora escorted him into the house.

"Go to your room now, son, for a bit of peaceful contemplation."

"I'll go, but I don't reckon I know what *conalation* is, Momma."

"*Con-tem-pla-tion*. It means to think on things. You know, how you might want the rest of your day to go."

"Well, I reckon I'll think about it goin' jus' as fine as apple pie."

She ruffled his hair. "Go. Rest."

"Yes'um."

Once Doc's wagon was out of sight, Ramsey turned and stood at the door, his shoulder against the frame. "So it's decided. I'll be leaving with the boys in the morning."

Cora stirred the kettle of beans on the stove top. "It was decided long before the doctor got here, Ramsey." She shimmied past him, outside. "I'll get that tea and some more bandage strips ready for you to take."

He followed her to the yard. "Cora. Cora, talk to me."

She kept walking. Nothing she had to say Ramsey Locke was interested in hearing.

It could be so perfect, but that was a pipe dream. Ramsey was content with the arrangement they had, except he'd like her to fulfill his physical needs, without a lasso around his neck. This gave Ramsey the freedom to do as he pleased without consideration to her well being. Maybe she was too critical. Ramsey made choices he felt would prosper the Lost C; leave a legacy for his son.

Treasure. He's the important one. His needs are what are of most concern. She agreed completely with that train of thought.

Cora opened the cellar door and descended the steps. She'd do whatever it took to make a home for Treasure. After all, she'd promised.

At supper Cora noticed the menfolk kept sneaking looks at each other. Treasure giggled now and then. "You want to tell me what's going on?" Cora finally asked.

"Think we should let your momma in on the secret, Treasure?" Ramsey asked.

"I reckon now'd be about the best time, Papa."

"Shorty, help Treasure and Calvin bring it in from the barn," Ramsey instructed.

Treasure about fell over his feet to hurry out of the house.

"Slow down thar, boy, 'fore you break a leg," Shorty said, joining the others.

"What secret is he talking about, Ramsey?" Cora asked.

"Hold on to your apron strings. You'll see."

In a few minutes, there was a clatter on the porch, and Shorty opened the door. Cora could not believe her eyes. A baby crib. Treasure held one side, and his smile threatened to split his face.

"Oh my goodness, what's this?" Her hand rested against her throat. Surprise caught her breath.

"What does it look like, Cora? It's a crib for the baby." Ramsey beamed. "We had some wood left over from the room add-on, and the boys, me and Treasure thought you might enjoy having a real bed for the little one."

She couldn't contain her tears. "A more wonderful gift I could never hope to receive." She went to touch the smooth sanded wood of the frame. "Thank you so much. All of you."

Treasure put his arm around his mother's skirt. "You think it's real purdy, Momma?"

Cora embraced him. "It's the most beautiful thing I ever laid eyes on. You did a splendid job, Treasure."

"Papa let me hammer a few nails, and I sanded on it too."

Ramsey stepped closer. "Treasure, can you go and make sure Shorty and Calvin get bunked down? Tell Rusty I'll relieve him on watch in a while. Take the extra lantern, so you can see to get back to the house."

"Yes'um."

The men took their cue and left, taking Treasure with them. When they'd gone, Ramsey picked up a package from the crib wrapped with brown paper and tied with a string. "I saw you eyeing this the other day, thought it'd be something to keep you busy while I'm gone."

Cora took the package he offered and opened it. Inside was the green print fabric she wanted to buy but couldn't afford. Beneath the fabric was a piece of flannel in red and blue plaid. "I don't know what to say, Ramsey. I...I...."

"You don't need to say anything, Cora. I wanted to buy it for you. Sorry, the colors of the blanket flannel aren't real baby-like, but Chester said it doesn't come in young'un colors."

"It'll do just fine, Ramsey, just fine." She gazed into his dark eyes, saw his soul reflected there. Kind. Compassionate. Loving.

In one stride he held her in his arms. She hadn't a second to protest. The truth was she didn't want to. His embrace consoled her fear. His heart beat against her neck as she rested her head on his chest. They connected, one with the other. "I'm pleased with your thoughtfulness," was all she could say.

"Cora, I don't want you to worry while I'm gone. It's not healthy for the baby. I wouldn't do anything that would put you and Treasure at risk of being alone, not on purpose anyhow. Can you hold the house together until I get back home?"

Tears stung her eyes. "I'll do my best, Ramsey. I'll be counting the days until we all can be together again. You, Treasure and me."

"Keep the rifle loaded and next to the door, in case. Extra shells are in the pantry behind the flour bin." He held her at arm's length. "I'm pretty sure you'll probably find some wild turkeys loitering around down by the creek. Shoot one and take it to the Hollisters', share Thanksgiving with them.

Cora shuddered. Sighed. "As you wish, Ramsey."

I'm sorry this trip comes so late in the year, and I'll miss the holiday with you and the boy. He cradled her chin in his fingers, raised it and kissed her. A soft, gentle kiss that asked for nothing in return. Ramsey splayed his hand firmly on the small of her back. "I like us being a family, Cora," he breathed into her ear. "I hope you know that."

Before she could respond, Treasure burst through the door. "Shorty said to tell you to hit the hay, Papa, 'cause sunrise better find them horses a good ways down the trail. He said Calvin will help keep watch over the string tonight, so no need for you to bother."

Cora pulled away. "Yes, Ramsey, you need to get a good night's rest. I'll take a supper plate out to Rusty, then Treasure and I will call it an evening too, so there won't be any goings-on to disturb you."

Ramsey dropped his hands to his sides, fists clenched. "I'll go to bed, but my thoughts most likely won't give way to sleep, Cora. You're mighty heavy on my mind tonight."

14

Five weeks had passed since Ramsey and the other men rode out for Abilene, Kansas. He and the trail hands ought to be within spitting distance of Rabbit Glen, almost home. Cora, with Treasure's help, had managed nicely until four days ago when the weather abruptly changed to winter, and the rain began. She turned her jacket collar against the wind and hurried to the barn.

Treasure ran to keep up.

"We need to find where your father stores the siding for the chicken coop and the planks that enclose the top. Those poor chickens will be swimming in another day with all this rain."

"I think I seen some big, flat boards in one of the stalls, Momma. Might that be them?"

Cora swung open the barn door. "Show me. Let's take a look."

Indeed Treasure was correct, but Cora knew she couldn't carry the large sheets of wood. Even with Treasure's help, it would be too much of a strain to risk. "We'll have to hitch the wagon and bring it around, see if we can scoot these up onto the tailgate and then slide them into the bed. They're much too heavy for us to lift, son."

"I'll fetch the team, and you bring the tack, Momma." Treasure ran to the far stall and opened the gate. "Easy, girls." He stood on a bucket, placed the head harness on each horse and led them outside.

By the time they hooked the horses to the wagon and drove it close to the barn door, they were drenched. It took nearly an hour to get the large panels loaded. The smaller planks used to cover the top of the wire coop were easier to manage.

Cora climbed to the wagon seat. "Yah, gitty up." She pulled the buckboard around the front of the house and halted near the chicken coop. "We'll get the top covered first, Treasure, that'll help to keep the hens dry until we can secure the sides."

"Yes'um." Treasure jumped out of the back of the wagon and began pulling with all his strength on one of the long planks.

"Here, son, let me help you."

Exhausted, Cora positioned the last board on top of the chicken coop and wired it into place. She shivered in the cold rain and worried that Treasure might become ill from exposure. They slid the larger pieces from the wagon to the ground, but she didn't have the strength to set them upright. "How about some lunch before we tackle the rest of this, Treasure?"

The boy gazed at the sky in the same way Cora had seen Ramsey do many times since she'd arrived at the Lost C Ranch.

"See the sun tryin' to peek through them clouds?" Treasure said. "Reckon we might get a break in this rain 'fore long." He pulled his water-soaked coat around him. "Could sure use a few sunny days to dry out some."

Cora put her arm around the boy and smiled. "Let's go inside, dry out by the fire and have some beans and cornbread. We'll need our strength to lift those side boards and secure them."

Inside, she placed their jackets on the corners of a chair back and scooted it near the woodstove to dry. At the table, neither spoke but ate what warmed their bellies and waited for the rain to slow. It never did. Cora hoped Ramsey might be back by this time. They'd figured three weeks to go to Abilene and less time to get back. She'd scanned the north ridge every day for the last week, yet the men hadn't returned.

The sky darkened more every hour, and Cora knew she and Treasure had to finish their task soon. "Finish that bowl, Treasure. We've got to venture back outside and get the chickens sheltered before the weather gets worse and we lose daylight."

They wired up the last side panel when in the distance Cora caught sight of movement. A rider on horseback, as near as she could tell. Her heart leaped with joy. Ramsey was home at last. She stood, Treasure at her side waiting until he got closer. When finally she had a better view, she saw the horse wasn't Ramsey's Appaloosa.

"Miss Cora, get yerself in out of this weather," the man yelled, as he rode toward the yard.

"Shorty, is that you? Where's Ramsey and the others?" Cora took a couple of steps further into the yard to meet up with the rider when a flash of lightning zigzagged across the darkened sky. Electricity filled the air, made it static and frightening. "Treasure, get to the house right this minute," she ordered. She turned the boy and gave him a gentle shove.

"What about you, Momma?" he called back.

"I'm right behind you...go on now."

Cora cupped her hands around her mouth. "Shorty put your horse in the barn and come to the house," she yelled. "I'll have a hot cup of coffee for you."

"Sure could use one," he hollered back.

Cora rushed to the safety and dryness of the cabin. Her clothes were drenched, as were Treasure's. "Go put on some dry clothes before you catch your death," she told him.

She knew she would not have time to change before Shorty came to the house, so she stood for a few minutes in front of the woodstove, fanning her skirt to help it dry. When she heard Shorty coming up the steps, she poured hot coffee into a cup and dished up a bowl of beans from the kettle on the cook stove. She sat it on the table along with a cold slice of cornbread.

"Thank ya, ma'am. I'm wet to the bone and hungry as a trapped varmint."

Cora pulled out a chair and sat. "Shorty, where are the others? Why isn't Ramsey with you?"

Shorty shoveled a few spoonfuls of beans into his mouth and took a swig of coffee before he answered. "Well, Miss Cora, when we got the stock to the railhead, that Army man said he'd buy 'em, but he couldn't pay us but two-fifty a head. Seems he was only authorized to pay top dollar for the first three hundred head that came in. Since we was behind gettin' thar, we ended up the short stick."

He ate half a piece of cornbread. "There was this fella thar, a man by the name of Carson. Said he had a second string of horses to bring in, but some of his crew had up and took off once they got paid for ridin' in the first bunch." He drunk more coffee. "Sure is tasty brew, Miss Cora."

"Shorty, please continue, tell me why Ramsey isn't here." Cora leaned in close, anxious.

"Well, ma'am, the army payin' us two dollars fifty cents a head, that weren't near what we'd figured on gettin'. For sure, the boss expected a whole lot more, and he was purdy put out over that fact."

"Oh, dear," Cora remembered Ramsey calculated how splitting the money between him, and the other two, would net his part enough to get through the winter, buy a few extra head of cattle for the spring drive. Less income would not accomplish what he'd hoped.

"Well, this fella, Carson, he helped make up the slack. He offered twelve dollars to anyone who'd ride with him, fetch the rest of his horses and herd 'em back to the railhead to sell 'fore that Army fella left. Ramsey, Rusty, and Calvin took 'em up on it," Shorty explained.

"And you, Shorty, you didn't want in on the windfall?"

"To tell you the truth, Miss Cora, I'm a whole lot older than the others, and my back was about to break in the saddle by the time we got there. I wasn't hankerin' to spend an extra two or three weeks ridin' stock, 'fore I could head back this direction."

Cora stood, her heart aching. "So Ramsey will be gone for three more weeks or longer?"

"He's hopin' not. Wasn't sure jest how far out of town this fella had his second string corralled. He said with the short pay from the Army, he couldn't pass up the chance for extra cash."

"I guess I can understand that." A sharp pain assaulted Cora's low back, caught her breath. She held to the kitchen counter for support waiting for the discomfort to subside. She'd overdone today. She needed to put her feet up for a bit.

"Could I get another cup of coffee, Miss Cora? Sure tastes good on a day like this'n."

Cora filled Shorty's cup, returned the pot to the stove and sat down. "So, you'll be heading back into town in the morning? Reckoned you want to rest up here tonight."

"Be obliged, ma'am. I'm pretty tuckered out and surely would like a few hours out of the saddle, if'n I could." He gulped down the coffee. "Ramsey did ask me to fill the stalls with fresh hay, and get the chickens closed in. I seen you and the boy got the chicken coop done already."

"Yes." Cora rubbed her hand against her swollen belly. "Why couldn't you have shown up yesterday, Shorty?"

"I was wonderin' why you couldn't have waited until tomorry when I'd be here."

She looked up and saw the twinkle of humor in the old man's eyes. She laughed. He laughed too.

Out of the blue, Cora realized Treasure hadn't come to the table, nor had she heard a peep out of him. "Excuse me, Shorty. I need to check on Treasure."

She stood in the doorway of his room, smiling. He was half on and half off his bed, his wet clothes scattered on the floor. A pair of dry long johns clung to one leg and arm of the boy's body. He was sound asleep. Cora gently moved him onto the bed, stuck his bare leg and arm into the garment and covered him with a blanket. His day was over. She was more than ready to follow suit.

"He's sawing logs," she told Shorty. "He put in a man's work today. I don't know what I'd have done without him."

"He's a good young'un." Shorty got up and grabbed his hat off the peg near the door. "Reckon I'll be headed for the barn now, ma'am. Be up bright and early in the morning. If you can think of anything else you need done around the place, once I do the stalls, I'm happy to oblige."

"Thank you, Shorty. Maybe you could ride out to the east pasture and open the gate so the cattle can wander into the lower range. They'll need to take shelter among the trees near the creek if this weather turns worse."

"Ain't no problem, Miss Cora."

"Then I'll see you at breakfast."

Cora closed the front door and went to the bedroom. Her wet clothes hung heavy and humid in the heat of the house. Every piece clung to her body as she tried to disrobe. After pulling a nightshirt over her head, she sat her soaked shoes and stockings on a chair and placed it near the fire so they'd be dry in the morning.

She lay warm beneath the covers, wishing with all her heart Ramsey had been the one who'd returned today. She could understand his reasoning, but her heart yearned that he might have missed her and his son too much to stay away longer. *What an absurd notion.* He wouldn't miss her at all. She was nothing more to him than his son's caregiver. His cook and housekeeper. A convenient bed partner if he had a need he couldn't squelch.

Cora loved Ramsey Keaton Locke. She didn't know the moment when it'd happened, but it had. The trouble was, he didn't love her. He still pined over the woman he'd lost—his sweet Caroline. Cora believed she'd never fill that place in his heart, nor was there space for a new love to prosper. There was no point in wishing it different. She could decide to remain content in the role he allowed her to have in his life, or when her baby was born, she could leave.

"Leave and go where?" Cora said aloud to no one. As long as Ramsey offered her a place to stay, she'd stay. Treasure had asked her to be his surrogate mother. He loved her, and it was impossible to imagine life without him, and she knew Ramsey would never permit her to take him away. So, yes, she'd stay. She'd focus on gratitude for the kindness afforded her, and the sanctuary given. She'd love a man who would never love her. She'd hide her broken heart with a smile. *As you wish, Ramsey.*

Cora reached to turn down the lantern, but a sharp stab of pain in her back diverted her attention. This time it radiated all the way around to her stomach causing the muscles to tighten into a hard knot. "Ouch." She rubbed her hand over her hardened belly trying to the ease away the discomfort. Slowly it subsided. *A full night's rest, that's all I need.*

She reached for the lantern again, and a gush of warmth oozed between her legs. Cora threw back the quilt cover and pulled up her gown to look. "Oh God, no. It's too early." A sticky blood-tinged fluid stained her night clothes. It stuck to her thighs, and more flowed from her body. Not wanting to move more than necessary, she grabbed her wet petticoat from the bedside chair, wadded it up and shoved it between her legs. Instinct told her to position a pillow beneath her heels and prop them up on the footboard.

She cradled her stomach in her hands, soothed the little one inside with gentle strokes. "Wait, sweet baby. Please wait." Fear palpitated her heart; her breaths came shallow and quick. The bleeding and pain that raised her belly into a hard ball must stop. If the baby came now, so early—it would surely die.

15

*C*ora woke, relieved to see the bleeding she'd experienced the evening prior was minimal. She heated water, washed and dressed before Treasure awoke, or Shorty came out of the barn to get breakfast. The rain still poured, puddles formed in the yard where the ground could no longer absorb the moisture.

She knew she couldn't do some of the heavier chores needed to get the cattle ready for winter, so she planned to talk to Shorty, convince him to stay on a few more days. Cora prepared a list of things to tackle. She had Shorty gather wood from the barn in the wheelbarrow and stacked it on the porch in easy reach. Then Shorty and Treasure took the wagon loaded with hay and placed it beneath the cover of the pole barn in the lower pasture. The cattle would need extra to eat now that the meadow grasses were dying off. There was the need to heat tar and broom it over the joints on the metal roof of the cabin. She had to put a pan under one leak in the corner near the room addition. They'd need a break in the rain though before that task was possible.

As it turned out, Shorty stayed for a whole week. The rains stopped on the third day, and he was able to coat the roof on the fourth. Wood, draped with a tarpaulin to keep it dry, covered the entire porch except for a narrow path to get from the steps to the door. Cora would be able to manage until Ramsey got back home, maybe in ten days' time.

"I'll be headed on into town now, Miss Cora. Think yer set purdy well." Shorty mounted his horse and tugged his hat over his brow.

"I appreciate all you've done around the place," Cora told him

"Will ya come back for supper sometime, Shorty?" Treasure asked.

"Wild horses couldn't keep me away from your momma's cookin', boy. I'll see ya 'afore long."

Cora and Treasure watched their friend ride off down the road, out of sight. The blue of the morning sky began to fade to gray, and Cora knew the rain would soon return. "Come inside, Treasure, help me peel potatoes to make soup."

"Yes'um. Reckon we're in for another storm by the looks of them clouds."

"I figure by suppertime we'll have rain. Let's get in and shut the door, stay dry and snug, what do you say?"

Treasure walked into the cabin and shed his jacket. The rain came and with it colder temperatures. By evening the drizzle turned into icy beads of sleet. They didn't go out except to bring in wood from the porch to keep the fire going. Over the following days, chores were kept to a minimum. Treasure checked the mules and team horses in the barn daily while Cora gathered eggs.

Soon the child became restless, and it was all Cora could do to keep him occupied. She brought out a box of buttons and had him sort them by size and color. They practiced writing A, B, Cs. He'd start school in the spring, and she wanted him to know how to make his letters beforehand.

The days passed slowly, and increasingly Cora's energy waned. The baby changed position, and her stomach protruded in front like she had a bushel basket under her skirt. She carried the child much lower now. From talk she'd heard, that's what happened when your time was close. She had another six or seven weeks she figured, so maybe that was about the time a baby dropped, got quiet and settled in for birthing.

On Wednesday there was a reprieve from the adverse weather. The sun came out from behind the clouds for most of the day.

"Momma, can I get Sara out of the barn and ride her in the yard?" Treasure begged. "I bet she's near got cabin fever locked up in that stall all this time."

Cora ruffled his hair. "I expect you're right about that." She knew it was Treasure who was having trouble being cooped up. "Go get her. You can ride until I get lunch fixed."

"Thanks, Momma." He rushed out of the house to the barn.

A sharp pain raced across Cora's hips. Her back ached, had since yesterday. She scooted a chair and sat, propped her feet on the seat of another. She'd take this time to rest a bit. Treasure wouldn't mind a few extra minutes to ride the mule.

Ramsey would surely be back in a few days. He'd missed Thanksgiving. She knew he'd make sure to arrive home before Christmas. He wouldn't want his son to be without his father on that holiday. The Hollisters had announced the church would hold a turkey dinner Christmas afternoon for all the church members. Mary Lou requested she bake some apple pies to share. Luckily there was a basket of fall apples in the cellar. Cora had planned to boil them down and make jars of apple butter but guessed she could spare a few for Christmas pies.

One blessing the adverse weather offered was an excuse not to spend Thanksgiving with the Reverend and his wife, as Ramsey had suggested. Mary Lou would have bombarded her with questions as to Ramsey's whereabouts and when he'd return and why this and what that? Cora was not in a mood to oblige the inquisition. She'd made fried meat pies for the Thanksgiving meal that evening; afterward, she and Treasure settled down with a bowl of popped corn to read from the *Riverside Magazine for Young People.* They'd had a lovely Thanksgiving, even though Ramsey was missed.

Again, the pain radiated from her back, around her hips and to the center of her stomach. She felt the baby move, roll into a ball. Her belly lifted, grew taut and hard.

Once the tension subsided, her stomach relaxed. When nothing followed after a few minutes, she got up to make cornbread to go with the potato soup simmering on the stove. When the bread was baked, she called Treasure into the house.

"Go stand by the stove and warm up while I dish you a bowl of soup."

"My hands is freezin' cold, Momma. I reckoned Sara was happy to be back in the barn and lay down on some warm straw."

"Even though it's cold outside, she needs to get some exercise. She'll be thanking you for that, son."

"Yes'um."

After lunch, Cora got out the swatch of the flannel Ramsey had brought for her. She knew she needed to sit a spell, and she had an idea to keep Treasure occupied and quiet. "How would you like to help me make some blankets for the baby, Treasure?"

"I don't know nothin' about sewin'...don't reckon I want to neither."

She rolled the material out on the table. "I'll do all the sewing, but I could sure use some help with the cutting. Those big scissors are almost too heavy for me to work."

"I reckon I could do ya some cuttin'. Show me where you want the line." Treasure held the cutting tool in his small hand, working the handle back and forth.

Cora smoothed out the flannel. "See this red line in the plaid? Think you can follow that line from one end of the material to the other."

"This'n?" He pointed to the fabric.

"That's the one. Then when you get that done, cut across the blue line to the other side. Can you do that?"

He laid the scissors on the flannel and began to cut. "Ain't gonna be no chore, Momma."

She watched as Treasure cut as she'd instructed.

"How's that?" he asked when he'd finished.

"Good. Now we need to make individual blankets out of the pieces you've cut." She showed him what line in the design to cut next. "Now, lay that piece on top of the remaining fabric and cut another the same size. We should be able to get several blankets out of this one piece of flannel."

Treasure did the job given, taking his time to lay each cut piece on top of the remaining material, then cutting another square. When he'd finished cutting six small blankets from the red and blue flannel, his face lit up with a grin. "All done, Momma."

"You did a mighty fine job, son."

Cora turned the edges and hand stitched a hem on all four sides of the first blanket. While Treasure continued to profess he had no interest in sewing, he sat across from her and watched intently as the needle went in and out, making small stitches all around.

Night came, the sky remained clear, stars shone, but the air was frigid. Cora folded each little blanket and stacked them in the crib, along with the baby gowns she'd made and the diapers she'd cut. All was ready now, even though these things weren't needed for a few more weeks.

She returned to the kitchen to help Treasure from the tub, covering him with a towel. She wanted him to be fresh and clean when his father got home. A good tub scrub would hold him for a week or more. Cora expected Ramsey back home by then.

With Treasure dressed in a clean pair of long johns, she had him help her drag the tub to the front door and out onto the porch, where she lifted it up to dump the water. When she did so, she felt the warmth of sticky liquid flow from her. Holding her legs close together, she hurried Treasure off to bed and went to her sleeping room to check herself.

She was wet, but the fluid was clear. Instinct told her she'd need to get into bed and stay there to keep the baby from coming early. She undressed, washed and put on a gown. As an afterthought, she went to the porch and cut a large square of the canvas that covered the wood. If she continued to leak, she didn't want to stain the bed coverings or the mattress.

Once prepared, she climbed beneath the covers. Recline, rest; she'd be all right. A sizable number of hours' sleep would offer a remedy. Like before when she'd bled a little, one night in bed fixed everything.

Cora drifted off to sleep with that thought.

It was the sound of her own voice that woke her. High pitched groans, neared to screams. Her back felt as if someone had rolled a wagon on it. Her stomach was hard, and the pain intense. *Oh God, the baby, it's going to come.*

She knew there was no holding it back this time. She'd have to do this alone, so she took inventory of what was needed close at hand. There was always a kettle of water on the stove. As soon as there was a lull in the pain, she'd fill a pot with hot water, cover it with a lid to hold the heat and grab a washcloth and towel. Somehow she'd managed to get from the bedroom to the kitchen and complete these tasks. She wasn't sure her strength would endure returning to her bed. When she picked up the pot to carry it to the sleeping room, another pain gripped her body, and she doubled over. More liquid oozed and clung to the insides of her legs.

"Momma, what's wrong, are ya sick?"

Cora glanced up. Treasure stood in the doorway of his room; worry lines creased his brow. His eyes clouded with fear.

"No, honey, I'm fit. I'm pretty sure I'll have my baby tonight, though."

"Do ya need me to help? Wash your face like you did when Papa was in the sick bed?"

She managed to set the pot dangling precariously from her fingers on the kitchen counter, then grasp the edge, bracing against the contraction that again assaulted her. When it ended, she told Treasure, "You can carry this pot of water into my bedroom and place it on the floor near the head of the bed."

Treasure did as instructed. "Now whatcha need done, Momma?"

"There's one thing that would be a real big help, son."

"I'll do anything ya ask me. Remember, Papa said I was the man of the place 'til he gets back."

"Yes, that's right, but having a baby, well, that's woman's work. The men mostly just have to stay out of the way so we can get it done." Cora smoothed his hair back from his forehead. "I need you to go back to your room and stay there, no matter what."

She struggled to walk him back to bed and tuck him beneath the covers. "Treasure, sometimes getting a baby out is painful. You might hear me moan, but know it's only part of the birthing. Nothing to worry about, so you stay put. Understand?"

"Yes'um."

Cora kissed his forehead. "If I need help, I know right where you are. I'll come fetch you."

"You can wake me up if'n I'm sleepin' Momma."

"That's a comfort to know, Treasure." Cora tucked the covers around him and left the room.

Hours passed, and the pain became unbearable. Cora drifted in and out of consciousness. Something was wrong. She could feel the baby right at the point of emergence, but it wouldn't come. She was bleeding a lot. Too much. The loss of blood made her weak and incoherent.

Ramsey, where are you? I need you. Help me.

The bedroom door cracked open. "Momma? I knocked but guess you didn't hear me." Treasure took a step into the room. "I heard ya cryin' out, Momma. I got me a worry on about ya."

Cora managed to raise her head off the pillow. "Go back to bed, son."

He walked in and stood at the end of the bed. "I don't know nothin' about how a woman births a baby, Momma, but my heart's tellin' me you're in a bad way. If Papa was here, he'd already have gone to fetch Doc Olson. I know it."

Treasure sat on the side of the bed and patted his mother's arm. "Bein' I'm the man of the house 'til Papa comes home, I reckon, it's my job to go get the doctor."

Cora noticed Treasure was wearing his winter jacket and his laced boots. "Why are you dressed? You should be in bed. I'm going to be all right, surely I will." Cora squeezed Treasure's hand, reassuring him. "Some babies take longer to arrive than others, is all. Remember, that's why Doc was late the day he came to check on your Papa?"

Treasure stood and took a couple of steps backward. "Momma, I reckon I'll get a whuppin' when you get to feelin' better, but I'm a-goin' to get Doc. You're lookin' mighty poorly."

Cora managed to rise on one elbow. "No, Treasure, I won't allow it." It was at that moment she heard icy pellets pound against the window. "It's sleeting outside, and it's not yet daylight. I won't have you going anywhere, young man." Cora hardly had the strength to speak. "Go back to your room this minute."

"I'm a-goin', Momma. Papa would 'spect no less bein' the cause."

She could see there was no way to talk Treasure out of what he deemed his duty, but perhaps she could convince him to do a task that would keep him out of harm's way.

"Treasure, this is what I want you to do. Ride old Sara down to the Hollisters' place. Request the Reverend to ride on into town and fetch the doctor. His bay horse will get there much faster than Sara ever could. Ask Mary Lou to come and help me birth my baby. If you'll do that I'll get help right away. It's the best plan, don't you think?" She held her breath, hoped he'd see her reasoning.

"I reckon that'd be a good idea, all right. It's real hard to get a mule into a trot."

"Yes, that's right. You're a smart young man." Cora felt another contraction coming fast after the last one. "You go now, do as we planned."

Before the contraction took her breath, she managed one last instruction. "Treasure, stay at the Reverend's house with Henry and Priscilla until Mary Lou returns home. Promise me, so I don't have to worry about you."

"Yes'um, I promise." Treasure pulled his cap onto his head and ran out of the house.

In a few moments, she heard him yell to Sara, "Gitty up girl, go fast."

When the onset of pain subsided, Cora leaned forward, pulled the covers away to assess her situation. Blood. There was so much blood. She sensed the baby struggled to come out, but as hard as she pushed, it wouldn't. She reached her hand downward, tried to feel if there was anything she could do to assist the birth, but before she'd completed the task another jolt ripped through her body. She fell back against the pillow and gritted her teeth against the scream she couldn't contain.

In the distance, thunder rolled, an expression of her torment. Lightning cracked, hitting something close by. A tree? The barn? Another flash lit up the room like a hundred torches.

"Treasure," Cora whispered. *Oh, dear God, why did I allow a little boy to go out in this storm?*

Cora drifted, went to that hazy dimension where she felt no pain. Even in her foggy state, she knew one thing for certain. If she didn't get this baby out soon, if she lost more blood, Ramsey would have to raise Treasure on his own.

16

amsey pulled the slicker tight about his neck. The rain hadn't let up for hours, his legs were soaked, his boots wet and his feet cold. He could hardly hold the reins, his gloved hands nearly frozen from the steady downpour of ice-spiked rain. If he pushed he'd be home by early morning, but common sense told him he needed to find a place of shelter, build a fire and warm himself.

He turned the Appaloosa off the trail and headed cross country toward the village fashioned amongst several cave-like openings in the side of Haunted Wolf Mountain. Hawk Feather would allow him to rest and warm himself in his dwelling. This route was a bit of a detour, but once he got to the village, he'd be a half day's ride from the cabin. He'd leave at first light.

Ramsey neared one of the caves and saw the glow of a small campfire. He approached cautiously although aware his presence was already sensed. "Hawk Feather, you sorry ass excuse for a renegade. You awake in there?"

An Indian man and woman appeared at the cave opening. The woman smiled. The man spoke. "Ramsey, you nearly got your butt shot off. I got some sharp arrows in my stash."

"With your aim, Sorry, I don't figure I have much to worry about." Ramsey dismounted. "Can I warm by your fire tonight? I'm near froze to death."

"We've got coffee over the flame, come in and sit," Hawk Feather's wife said.

Sorry and Ramsey sat cross-legged at the fire's edge and chatted for several hours, catching up on the news of each of their families.

"I saw your woman was big with child, Ramsey, when my sons and I brought you rabbits a few weeks back. Didn't know you had it in ya." Hawk Feather laughed and slapped Ramsey on the back.

"Was a bit surprised myself." For some reason, he couldn't explain, Ramsey chose not to disclose the baby Cora carried was not his. "I was hoping to make it back to the cabin by morning, but this rain slowed me down a parcel. I figure if I can dry my boots here tonight, I'll head out at daybreak. Be home by noon."

"Here is a sleeping fur," the woman offered. "Make a place over there." She pointed to a flat area just beyond the circle of firelight. "I'll fill your belly before you leave tomorrow."

"Thank you, Butterfly Woman. Your hospitality is appreciated."

Ramsey took the bear fur and spread it as instructed. Hawk Feather and his wife retired to the other side of the cave, and all became quiet except for the crackle of the fire.

The warmth of the fur surrounded Ramsey, and it took only a moment for his tired body to relax into a deep sleep. His last thoughts were of Cora—getting back to her and his son. He'd come to love the woman. He reckoned he had since their first meeting when she'd squared her shoulders, stated her name and her purpose for coming to the Lost C. She never backed down from what she had to do, and he liked that kind of feminine power. As much as he wanted to tell her, every time he thought to, guilt riddled his resolve, as though he was betraying Caroline. He'd held back. Now he knew he had to tell her. Give her his heart.

Ramsey didn't know how long he'd slept when his eyes flew open. Had someone called his name? He looked around the cave interior. Hawk Feather and Butterfly Woman slept sound. The night was still, surreal. A faint voice floated through the air. "Ramsey, my sweet Ramsey."

He rose on his elbow and there above the glowing embers of the fire was an image, a shimmering white apparition. He couldn't believe what he saw. "Caroline... my God, is that you?"

He rubbed his eyes, looked away, then back. The image lingered. As he watched it materialize completely, there was no doubt it was Caroline.

"Ramsey, you must not stay," she said. "There's trouble. You're needed at home. Go now, before it's too late."

"What? What do you mean?" he stammered. But before he got an answer, the image faded and disappeared. His heart pounded, crushing his ribs. There was no air to breathe. "Cora. Oh, Lord, it's Cora." *Something is wrong.*

The two friends, awakened by Ramsey's yelling, got up from their bed, the look in their eyes questioned his sanity.

"Butterfly Woman, Sorry, I must leave," Ramsey said, jumping from his bed."

"Look at this weather. It's still raining and cold." Hawk Feather stared at his friend, confused. "It's hours yet before daylight."

"I don't have time to explain, I just know I must get home as fast as I can. Cora and Treasure are in danger. I feel it in my bones."

Butterfly Woman picked up the fur pallet from the floor and drew it around Ramsey's neck, securing it with a piece of rawhide. "This will help keep you dry and warm. It will benefit no one if you arrive and have death on your coattail, Ramsey Locke."

"Thank you, both, my dear friends." He left the warmth of the cave, mounted his horse pulled his hat low and turned toward the wind. He spurred the Appaloosa and headed down the trail, southeast, toward Rabbit Glen.

Adrenalin kept Ramsey alert as he rode home. The horizon turned lighter over Washoo Ridge, but the sun remained hidden behind the high fog bank. The rain had momentarily stopped, yet the gloominess of the day gave no promise that it would stay that way for long. In the distance, Ramsey caught sight of the cabin. No wisp of smoke curled above the chimney. *Why hadn't Cora kept the fire stoked?* The fact that she hadn't confirmed the dread that consumed him. Once on flat ground, he slapped his reins against the Appy's flanks and raced full bore toward the house. The barn door stood wide open. Another sign something was amiss.

Ramsey slid from the saddle, flipped the reins around the hitching post, and burst through the door. "Cora, Treasure, where are you?"

No one answered. He glanced into Treasure's room and found his bed rumpled, but the child was gone. *He's crawled in with Cora, with the house so cold.* No, Treasure would have stoked the fire, if he was able. *Oh, Jesus.*

He rushed to the sleeping room. Cora lay against the pillow her face pale as watered milk, her eyes like she'd been in a bar fight and lost. The bed quilt was covered with blood. Ramsey's knees buckled. "Cora. My darling Cora, what's happened?" He knelt at her side.

Her eyes fluttered half open. "Ramsey, you've come. I needed you so desperately, and you've come." She closed her eyes again, took a ragged breath. "The baby, I can't get it out. We are both dying."

"No. You hear me, Cora. You will not die." Ramsey panicked only a moment. He knew what to do. Deliver this baby. He'd vowed to step away from his life as a physician, but now he drew upon his professional training to right this situation. To save Cora and her unborn child.

In his short medical career, he'd never delivered a baby, but he'd been trained to do so and had assisted his midwife mother several times. *They say you never forget what you've learned; the trick is to be able to recall it to mind.*

Ramsey closed his eyes, conjuring the image from long ago. "Cora, I have to look. See what's wrong, why the baby hasn't come yet."

"Do what you must. Help me, Ramsey, please."

He pulled back the blanket and lifted her blood-soaked gown, pushing her knees apart. "It's breach."

"What does that mean?" Cora whispered.

"It's coming butt first, Cora. I've got to try and turn the infant so I can get hold of its feet and coax it out."

Ramsey placed a hand on Cora's stomach. "When your next contraction fades, I'm going to have to push the baby back into the birth canal a little. It's going to hurt, Cora, and I'm sorry, but it must be done."

"Nothing could hurt any worse than what I've already experienced." Cora attempted to raise a hand and wave him on, but she couldn't hold it up long enough to complete the gesture.

"All right, darlin', here we go." When Cora was between contractions, which was only a few seconds, Ramsey pushed on the baby's bottom until it retreated behind the feminine opening, then with his fingers, he found the baby's legs and pulled them downward.

"Oooooh, God, get it out. Get it out now. I'm ripping apart. Oooooh." Cora cried, then passed into momentary unconsciousness.

When Ramsey saw the two tiny feet protrude from the birth channel, he gently pulled, and the baby slid from its mother. The infant, a girl, was pale, her tiny mouth blue. Her circulation had been compromised in the arduous labor. Luckily the cord had not wrapped around the baby's neck, probably its saving grace, Ramsey figured. He cut the cord, lifted the baby, and smacked her on the bottom. Nothing. Again, he smacked the newborn, and she uttered a gurgling squeak of protest. He took the corner of a muslin diaper, secured it around his finger and swabbed the baby's mouth, going as far down the throat as he could, causing a gag reflex in the child. A wad of mucus came up, and he quickly removed it with the cloth. The tiny baby let out a cry in earnest. She was breathing and turning pink—all good signs. Ramsey laid the baby next to her exhausted mother and wrapped part of the sheet around her. "You have a beautiful little girl, Cora." The tiny infant nuzzled against the warm breast that offered a familiar scent.

"Is she all right? Healthy?" Cora struggled to speak.

"She's perfect. You can rest easy now."

Cora cradled the baby close in her arms, breathed a sigh and drifted off to sleep. The baby girl sucked her fist and cooed.

In the kitchen, Ramsey stoked the fire, took what little hot water was left in the kettle and poured it into a pan. He ladled cool water from the drink bucket into the hot to produce a tepid bath. Back in the sleeping room, Ramsey quickly washed the blood from the baby with a clean cloth then dressed her in one of the gowns Cora had stitched. Securing the infant in one of the blue and red flannel blankets, he laid her again next to her mother.

"I'm going to clean you, Cora, and the bed."

She moaned her acknowledgment.

He took another cloth, washed Cora, disposed of the afterbirth and put fresh linens beneath her. He fashioned a pad to catch any remaining blood flow, hoping that wouldn't be much. She'd lost too much already.

Ramsey needed to rouse Cora fully awake, ask about Treasure. Perhaps the Reverend and Mary Lou had come and taken him to their house. But why hadn't Mary Lou stayed to help Cora? A chill pebbled his flesh.

He gently washed Cora's face with warm water. "Cora, wake up and meet your daughter. She's a beauty, got a head full of golden hair, and she's no bigger than a minute."

"The baby, it's here?" Cora strained to open her eyes. "It's alive?"

She hadn't remembered asking about the condition of the baby before. Ramsey wasn't sure she was, even now, fully aware. "Look at your little girl." He slid his hand beneath the baby and held her up so Cora could get a better view. The baby squirmed, put a tiny fist to its mouth. One eye opened a slit as if attempting to survey her new world.

"Thank you, Ramsey. We would have both died if you hadn't come."

Cora gazed about the room. "Where's Doc Olson? He should have been here long ago."

"What are you saying? Did you send Treasure to fetch the doctor?" His voice cracked.

"He sensed something wasn't right, Ramsey. I couldn't talk him out of going. He was determined to take the action he knew you would have under the circumstances." Cora took a labored breath. "I did put my foot down, told him he couldn't ride Sara all the way into town."

"The barn door is open, and he's not here, so I reckon that means he went against your wishes. Darn fool kid." Ramsey got up, ran his hand through his hair.

"He did go, Ramsey, but I made him promise he'd only ride as far as the Hollisters'." Cora stopped again, caught her breath. "I told him the Reverend could fetch the doctor faster on horseback than he could riding a mule. He promised." Cora's eyes widened, fear sparked.

"I instructed him to stay with Henry and Priscilla and ask Mary Lou to come help with birthing the baby. Oh God, Ramsey, I'm sure Mary Lou would have come, been here long ago if Treasure had gotten the message to her." She began to cry. "Something's happened to him, and it's my fault. I let him leave."

The rain doused harder against the windows and lightning streaked across the morning sky. "What if Treasure was struck by a bolt? What if he's dead?" Cora sobbed.

"You stop that kind of talk, woman. He did what he thought he needed to do, no matter what you might have told him otherwise. I doubt tying him to the porch would have held him here when he knew you needed help. If it's anyone's fault, it's mine for not coming on home once we sold those ponies to the cavalry. If I'd been here, none of this would've played out."

Ramsey made sure the blankets were snug around Cora and the baby. He brought two chairs from the kitchen, turned their backs toward the bed, to be sure if Cora did fall asleep, relax her grip on the baby, it wouldn't roll off the bed. "I'm going to the Reverend's, see if Treasure's there. Maybe Doc's doing some other doctoring that's urgent, and that's why he hasn't made it yet. And, if one of the Hollister young'uns is sick, Mary Lou wouldn't have left 'em alone while the Reverend went to fetch the doctor." Ramsey offered words of comfort he didn't believe. He slipped on his still-damp coat. "I'll be back as soon as I can. You stay put in that bed, keep the little one warm."

"Hurry, Ramsey. Go find our son and bring him home."

Ramsey rode like a Texas tornado in June, reached the Hollister house as they sat down for breakfast.

"Come in Ramsey, have a cup of coffee and some biscuits with us," Mary Lou said when she opened the door to find her neighbor there. "You on your way home from sellin' your stock?"

Ramsey didn't answer Mary Lou. "Is Treasure here?"

"Why, no, dear. Is he supposed to be?" She put her hand to her chest; her eyes told Ramsey she sensed the seriousness of his visit.

He explained all that had happened and asked the Reverend if he'd fetch the doctor and take him to see about Cora and the baby.

"Mary Lou, can you go to the cabin, sit with Cora until Doc Olson gets there. She's been alone through this whole ordeal. She almost died. The baby, too."

"Yes, of course, I'll go right away. Priscilla, watch after your brother," she told her daughter while she wrapped a heavy shawl about her shoulders and put a hat on her head.

"I'll hitch the team for the Missus, Ramsey, then head right on into town to find Doc Olson. What are you going to do?" Reverend Hollister asked.

"I'm going to find my son. He never made it to your place, so he's got to be somewhere in between. If the rain and lightning scared old Sara, she might have bucked him off. He's been out there all night, Reverend. He's alone. He's only six years old and the night's cold enough to freeze a grown man to death.

Unchecked tears trickled down Ramsey's cheeks. "I just got used to having a son...I can't lose him now."

"Go, Ramsey. I'll join up with you in the search as soon as I get word to Doc Olson. In the meantime, I'll pray for the boy's safety."

Ramsey opened the door to leave. He paused. "I hope your prayers, and mine, are answered today, Reverend. If anything bad has happened to my son, God and I won't ever be talking again."

17

amsey and Reverend Hollister walked out of the house together. "Soon as I get Mary Lou in the wagon, I'll head to town and get word to Doc Olson."

"Much obliged." Ramsey put his foot in the stirrup and rose to the saddle.

"When I get back, I'll catch up to you," the reverend said.

Setting his hat low over his brow, Ramsey nudged the Appaloosa forward. "I'll start back towards the cabin, but off the road a ways toward the creek, in case the boy got thrown." He turned his collar up against the dampness of the morning mist. "You take the other side of the road when you return. If I'm not back at the house with my boy in tow by the time you get there, start back this way. We'll meet up somewhere in the middle."

"I'll do that Ramsey. We'll find him. He's probably hunkered down next to a big oak cussin' Sara for tossin' him off and runnin' away. Reckon he's sittin' there waiting for the day to brighten so he can see his way back home."

"Reckon," Ramsey said hoping it would prove out the fact.

He heeled his horse and rode off into the unusually thick fog. The heavy shroud hovered about three feet off the ground and made it seem as though you were half in one world and half in another. The sun, imprisoned above the dense shelf, made a valiant effort to break free but succeeded only in giving the morning a moldy green hue.

Ramsey squinted his eyes trying to discern the way off the main road and down the embankment toward Weaver Creek. Every footfall of his horse, every crack of a twig beneath the big Appaloosa's hooves echoed in his ears, as though trapped inside a bubble whose perimeters he couldn't see.

"Easy, girl," Ramsey cautioned when the Appaloosa skidded on the damp ground. "Easy."

One slow step at a time the horse found her way to the bottom of the ravine, which lay nearly six feet below the main road. The fog, less dense here, allowed Ramsey to ride the creek bed and see the embankment as well. There was no possibility he'd miss spotting Treasure if he'd fallen somewhere in between.

"Treasure? Son, can you hear me?" he called.

An eerie silence was the only reply. Not even a bird chirped in the trees, nor could Ramsey hear any critter scurrying about in the underbrush. A chill snaked his spine, and his heart constricted, shielding against what he might discover.

"Treasure," he yelled. "You're not in any trouble, boy. Call out, so I can find you."

Again, no response.

He'd ridden a half mile or so when he hit a patch of extreme fog. The mist laced through the trees along the creek and settled near the ground. Ramsey couldn't see more than a few inches beyond his horse's nose. He moved slow, cautious, and desperate. He could no longer see the grade of the road above.

"Treasure, where are you?"

He followed the edge of the creek bed. There was an abundance of water rushing over the rock-strewn gully due to the recent rains. He maneuvered the Appy steadily in the direction of the cabin, calling Treasure's name every few minutes. It seemed like he'd ridden for hours, the strangeness of the day made his movements fuzzy, disconnected. As near as he could figure, he was still a mile or more out from the east pasture fence.

The damp air swirled around him, covered his face with beads of moisture and weighted his eyelashes. He wiped his eyes with his hand and resumed his search. Several yards ahead, he caught a glimpse of a faint glow. Was that finally the sun peeking through?

Ramsey blinked several times. It wasn't sunlight; he was sure of that now, but what? Tapping the Appaloosa in the sides, he picked up the pace and headed toward the light. "Hollister, is that you ahead?" Ramsey figured the reverend had stopped at his place and grabbed a lantern. A smart move. *Wish I'd had the forethought.* Damn. Hollister was supposed to be searching on the opposite side of the road. Surely he'd not had time to complete a sweep of that area yet. Then it hit him. *Maybe the reverend found Treasure, is coming to give me the news.* Relief coursed through Ramsey's veins like warm cider.

"Reverend, I see ya. Stay put, I'm headed your way," he yelled.

The glow beyond remained steady as Ramsey rode toward it, yet he kept vigilant the search for Treasure along the creek bank, in case what he hoped didn't prove to be the fact. Getting closer to the source of the light, he could see an image of sorts, but it didn't appear to be that of the Reverend. Who in the hell would be out in this fog if they didn't need to be?

He wound his way around two large boulders and approached the illuminated image. "Caroline?" She'd come to him again. Had she not appeared at the cave, Cora and the baby would most likely be dead. Caroline had warned him of trouble. *Can it be...?*

"Ramsey, my love, you have not lost your mind. It is truly me you see," she said. "I have good news, dear one. What you search for is here." She turned, raised her arm and pointed. The radiance from her body lit the area. There on the ground, sprawled half in the creek, lay Treasure.

Ramsey jumped from the saddle, ran to the unconscious boy and cradled him in his arms. His clothes were wet and his skin cold to the touch. He was breathing slow, shallow breaths. "Son, everything's gravy now. I'm here, Treasure. I'm going take you home."

"I've been watching over him, Ramsey dear until you came." The otherworldly Caroline stood near.

"Thank you for that." Ramsey stared at the image of a woman he'd once loved. His heart pained, his breath labored. "And thank you for the warning of trouble when I slept by Hawk Feather's fire."

"You were able to save the woman?"

"Yes. She survived and her infant as well."

"*Her* infant, Ramsey?"

"I'm not the father, Caroline."

"Oh, sweet Ramsey. You may not have planted the child-seed, but that doesn't mean you can't step into the role of the little one's father. Think on these words I've spoken."

He rubbed his hands robustly up and down Treasure's back, getting his circulation going again. "I must get my son home, to the warmth of the fire."

Caroline glided over the ground and lingered a foot from them. "I'm at peace, Ramsey. It's time you were also. You have this handsome child to raise, and a new babe to take into your life."

She appeared thoughtful for a moment. "You have a wife. She loves you, Ramsey."

Ramsey stood, holding Treasure in his arms. "She does? How could you...?"

"The spirit world knows many things mortals have no understanding of, but this you can comprehend, my dear one." She floated lower to the ground. "I say this to you now, Ramsey. Take your son, go home to your wife and baby, open your heart to love and live the wonderful life gifted to you."

"But, Caroline, I...I...."

"Dear, dear, Ramsey. I know you will never forget me, but memories are only that. They are not meant to halt our living, nor are they there to close our hearts against loving again."

The apparition shimmered just beyond Ramsey's reach. It radiated calm. "I want to love again, Caroline. I do."

"It is time for me to depart from this in-between place, but I cannot until I know you are ready to move on as well, Ramsey. Are you?"

"I am. I truly am."

"Then it is good between us." She glided across the ground, increasing the distance between them. "Go home, my love, rejoice in the life you can share with someone who loves you. Goodbye, Ramsey."

The glow that was Caroline receded further and further into the trees until Ramsey could no longer see it. A newfound peace flooded his being, and his heart ached to get his son safely home and to embrace his wife and daughter. He already thought of the baby as his. However, Cora might not allow it. Holding Treasure in one arm, Ramsey mounted the Appaloosa. He tucked the boy inside his jacket and headed up the embankment to the road toward home. He'd go out later and search for the mule. Sara wouldn't stray far from home if she'd survived the storm.

Beyond the holding pen, he saw the lights of home. The fog had lifted considerably. To the west, he saw a man on horseback riding in his direction. He recognized the hat.

"Locke. I was heading back to meet up with you." The Reverend yelled. "Thank God, you found the boy. How is he?"

"He's in poor shape but alive."

Reverend Hollister halted his horse. "Doc Olson should be at your place by now. He took right out as soon as I got word to him." He leaned over and put his hand on the limp child in Ramsey's arms. "He's got spit. He'll bounce back."

Ramsey nodded. "Reckon."

"Tell Mary Lou I've gone home to watch over our young'uns. The day looks like it'll clear soon, she'll have no trouble gettin' back to our place when she's ready. Have her stay as long as she's needed. I'll keep things intact at our place."

"I'll do that, Reverend. I need to get the boy on home now, get him into some dry duds."

"Be on your way. You're nearly at the back door."

Even though Ramsey wanted to give the Appaloosa free rein the remaining distance, he feared Treasure might have some injury inside. He didn't want to jostle him too much.

At last, he was in the yard. Ramsey dismounted with his son held fast and walked inside the house. Doc stood at the stove filling a bowl with hot water.

"Ramsey, you're home, and the boy's with you. Here, here. Put the child in his bed," Doc directed. He began to examine Treasure, and the boy roused a bit. Ramsey tugged off his wet clothes, and after he and Doc had surveyed Treasure's body for cuts and breaks, he put a pair of dry long johns on his limp body.

"Sa-ra, girrrl, gitty up." The boy mumbled incoherently.

Ramsey touched his son's cheek and sighed. He sure hoped Sara had survived the night.

Treasure drifted off again and curled into a ball.

"I'll get him under the blankets, Ramsey, and spoon-feed him some hot tea. That'll perk him up. I'll take care of things here. You go and tend to your wife," Doc encouraged.

Inside the sleeping room, Ramsey removed his coat and brushed off his pants. Mary Lou Hollister nodded, got up from the chair where she'd kept vigil and left the room. Ramsey went to the basin on the bed table and washed his hands, drying them on a muslin towel. He sat on the side of the bed. Cora was awake, and she smiled at him.

"May I hold the baby?" he asked.

"Of course. You delivered her, you certainly have a right," Cora took her arm from beneath the baby so Ramsey could lift her.

She was small and fragile, and his heart danced. He was this little girl's protector. She slept. He didn't know the color of her eyes, but he wanted to. Her tiny mouth curled into a smile. Dreaming, people said, when a baby so young did that. Ramsey wasn't sure he believed the tale. He wanted to believe she smiled to show her approval; that she felt secure in the comfort of his arms.

A few minutes later the doctor appeared in the doorway of the bedroom. "Nasty bump on his head," he announced. "Mary Lou is gettin' a second cup of hot tea down the boy, that'll warm his innards. He's a bit dizzy, got head pain I 'spect, but he's young and stout so don't think it'll pose a problem. Ramsey, you know to wake him every few hours when he's sleeping over the next couple of days, make sure he comes alert."

"Yes, Doc. I'll be sure he's talking and thinking straight."

Doc opened his black satchel and pulled out an official looking document. He rummaged again and retrieved a quill and ink bottle. "I'll file this with the recorder when I get to Sutter Springs next week."

He dipped the pen into the ink. "Let's see. Mother's name? That'd be Cora ...?

"Blythe," Cora provided her middle name.

"Cora Blythe Locke." Doc filled in a line on the form.

Cora felt a rush of embarrassment, although she didn't know why she should. That was her name.

"Father's name?" Doc asked.

Ramsey gazed at Cora. Could she read his thoughts? She smiled at him and nodded.

"Uh-hum." The doctor cleared his throat and asked again. "Father's name?"

"Ramsey Keaton Locke," Ramsey stated, his chest puffed.

A hint of a smile to curled Doc's mouth as he filled in the line. "That now leaves us with the baby's name. You got one picked out?"

"Odetta, after my mother," Cora stated.

"And is there to be a middle name?" Doc asked.

Cora rested her hand on Ramsey's arm. "Were you close to your mother?"

"Nadine," he whispered. Then louder he said, "Nadine."

"All right, let me be sure I got this down right. The baby shall be known as Odetta Nadine Locke. Is that correct?"

"Yes, Doc, that's her name." Cora lifted her head to meet Ramsey's brief kiss.

"A rightful name for our little girl." Ramsey kissed the baby's forehead, then leaned down and kissed his wife again. His eyes expressed the love held in his heart. He stroked a finger across Cora's cheek. "She's almost as beautiful as her mother."

Doc placed the paper and pen back into his bag. "I'll go sit with the boy awhile, break Mary Lou free to put some beans on to cook," he said, turning to leave.

"Tell Treasure I'll come see him as soon as I'm strong enough to get out of this bed, will you, Doc?"

"That'll be a few days yet, Cora, but I'll give Treasure your message." Doc left the room, pulled the door shut behind him.

Ramsey placed Odetta back in her mother's arms and lay down beside them on the bed. His son was going to be chipper in a few days, and Ramsey would find a way to reward Treasure for his bravery—for being a man in his stead.

He reclined on the bed and spooned against Cora's back, his arm across her waist. His hand caressed the tiny bundle suckling at her breast. He was home too—safe in the arms of the woman he loved.

18

Over the next five days, Ramsey found a new appreciation for women folk. How a woman with a newborn ever managed to keep up with, not only the baby chores, but the cooking, cleaning, and care of other children was beyond him. And, the lack of sleep, however, did they manage on so little shuteye?

He was worn slick maintaining the household duties, cooking meals for Cora and Treasure, who'd both been ordered to bed rest by Doc Olson. Cora pretty much took care of the baby, changing diapers and feeding Odetta. Ramsey gave the baby a daily wash and delighted in this special time with her, relished her bright blue eyes and quirky smiles. Treasure had been only allowed to peek at his baby sister from the doorway, and he was ranting to hold her and announce his standing as big brother.

Doc Olson was scheduled to stop by tomorrow and check on both his patients. Ramsey didn't want to hasten the necessary time for Cora and Treasure's healing, but he was sure hoping for a reprieve soon from the extra tasks.

"Papa, I'm hankerin' for a game of checkers. Can we play?" Treasure yelled from his room.

"Give me a minute, son. I'm up to my elbows in biscuit dough." Ramsey scraped the glob into a pan and placed it in the oven compartment of the wood stove.

The cabin door opened and Shorty walked in. "Got any coffee left in the pot, boss?"

Ramsey poured a cup and sat it on the table. "You've sure been a Godsend, partner, coming to help with the outdoor chores."

Shorty took a drink, swished it around in his mouth and swallowed. "Couldn't have things goin' astray around the place, with you a prisoner of the apron and all."

"Papa, are you comin'?"

"Be right there, son."

"The kid gettin' antsy?" Shorty asked.

"You have no idea." Ramsey pushed his hands through his hair. "I can understand though, getting a bit stir crazy myself. Shorty, how's our patient in the barn doing?"

"Reckon she's near mended, boss. Was makin' a helluva racket this mornin' wantin' her breakfast."

Ramsey grinned. "That's good news."

Reverend Hollister had come across Sara on his way home the night they searched for Treasure. Old Sara struggled to climb the embankment to the road, one eye injured and a nasty gash on her side, both injuries incurred from tumbling down the hill that night in the rain. She'd strayed over a mile from the site, confused and scared. The Reverend soothed her and coaxed her back to the barn at the Lost C. Once Cora and the baby were tended and Treasure asleep, Ramsey went to inspect the damage.

He'd made a paste of iodine and axle grease then applied the mixture to Sara's side. The eye couldn't be saved. He cleaned the socket the best he could, then placed a bandage strip he'd borrowed from Doc Olson, around the mule's head. "That'll keep the flies out," he'd told the Reverend.

"Thank God you could save her, Ramsey."

"Couldn't be any other way, Hollister. Had to spare my boy any further sorrow."

Ramsey shook the memory of days past and went to Treasure's room. "How'd you like some fresh air, boy? I got somebody in the barn who wants to say hello."

"Sara? Is she feelin' better?"

"Get some clothes on, and we'll go ask her."

Ramsey figured Doc would cut the boy loose when he came tomorrow, and Treasure seeing his friend was the healing balm he needed.

Inside the barn stall, Treasure stroked the mule's neck and laid his head against her shoulder. "We both got hurt, Sara, but looks like we're gonna mend jus' fine."

"Do you remember what happened, son?" Ramsey hadn't questioned until now.

"I was makin' Sara go as fast as she could. Out of nowhere a bolt of lightning struck that old oak near the bridge," Treasure said. "Sara stopped like she'd hit a fence and her feet got tangled in the brush alongside the road, and she started slidin' down the hill, Papa. I tried to hang on, but I couldn't and fell off somewhere along the way. I don't remember nothin' else until I woke up, Doc Olson pokin' my ribs." Treasure recounted the event.

"I did have a dream, Papa, while I was laying there in the mud. I dreamed I was in the snow and I was cold. The snow was so dang fierce I couldn't see to find my way home, so I hunkered down under a tree. I thought I was going to turn to ice right on the spot, Papa. Then this real purdy angel came. She put her wings all around me, and I warmed right up. I knew I wasn't gonna freeze so I took me a nap. Next thing I knew, I was home in my bed."

"It wasn't a dream, Treasure. There *was* an angel who came, and she kept you safe until I found you."

"A real angel?"

"Cross my heart." Ramsey made an X mark on his chest.

When night came, the chores finished, Treasure, Cora, and Odetta slept soundly. Ramsey collapsed into a chair at the kitchen table, a cup of leftover coffee in his hand. He folded his arms on the table top—he'd rest his head a minute, then drink the coffee and go to bed. He figured he'd have about three hours to sleep before Odetta woke up crying for a meal.

Still sprawled across the table, the coffee cold and untouched, pounding on the door woke Ramsey. He sleep-staggered to open it. "Doc. Come in. What time is it?"

"The cock crowed hours ago, Ramsey. Why ain't you got the bacon frying?" Doc glanced toward the wood cook stove. "No Arbuckles brewin'?"

"I'll get a pot going right away, Doc. I can't believe I never woke up during the night." Then the thought hit him. Cora, the baby, are they all right? He rushed to the sleeping room and found Cora fully awake, sitting up against the pillows. The baby suckled at her breast.

"She slept through the night. Isn't that amazing?" Cora's smile lit up the room.

"Reckon she'll be making a habit of that?" Ramsey mused. He walked over to the bed and brushed his finger lightly over Odetta's blonde curls. "You'll have to braid her hair before long."

"It'll probably all fall out, then come back with what her real color will be," Cora offered.

"No kidding?"

"That's what Mary Lou told me."

"She's had two babies, so she'd know."

Then Ramsey remembered. "Doc's here to check on you and Treasure. I'll send him in and get some coffee brewing. We're both in need of a cup. Would you like one?"

"I'd love a weakened cup with breakfast when it's ready. Thank you, Ramsey."

"Anything for my beautiful wife." He smiled.

Ramsey returned to the kitchen and found Doc and Treasure sitting at the table.

"The boy is fit as a fiddle. Don't let him play too hard for another few days, but he can handle doin' some chores," Doc announced.

"Doc Olson, I ain't so sure I'm up to doin' chores jus' yet," Treasure protested.

The doctor scratched his chin. "Then, in that case, I recommend another week of bed rest to get you back to par."

Treasure's eyes grew wide, his mouth agape. "Right this minute I felt me a spurt of better. I'm feelin' plumb full of vinegar, Doc Olson, I don't think them chores is gonna be no problem a'tal."

"Well, Treasure, that's mighty good to hear." Doc looked up at a grinning Ramsey and winked.

"Cora's awake, Doc. She's waiting for you. I'll have a hot cup ready when you're done checking her and the baby over," Ramsey stated.

"Papa, when am I gonna get to hold my baby sister? Heck, she'll be nearly growed if I have to wait much longer." Treasure gave a disgusted sigh. "I only seen her from a distance when she was sleepin' with momma."

Doc reached over and patted the boy's arm. "Why don't we let you do that right now, Treasure."

"It'd be all right?"

"Now's a perfect time," Ramsey said. "Your momma and Odetta are awake. Come on, let's see if you like her."

Ramsey opened the bedroom door for his son to have a look.

Cora reached out her arm. "Son, come give me a hug. I've been so worried about you."

"Papa told me you was stuck in the sick bed and couldn't come to look about me, but he's done a purdy fair job of it." Treasure walked over to the side of the bed.

"That gives my heart some ease." Cora put her arm around his waist. "Sit down, and I'll introduce you to your sister."

Treasure climbed onto the bed and sat crossed legged. Cora lifted the baby and placed her in his arms.

"This is Odetta Nadine," she said.

Treasure looked at the baby for a long time, his expression unreadable. Then he broke into a toothy grin. "That's a mighty big name they hung on you, sister. I don't think you're gonna be able to tote it 'til you grow some. I'm gonna call you Detty." He bent down and kissed his sister on the forehead. "Hello, Detty. I'm your big brother, Treasure."

Ramsey fought back the tears, encouraged by the tender moment between his children.

Cora lost the battle as tears of joy stained her cheeks.

"All right, young man, how about you return your sister to her mother. You and your pa skedaddle so I can do my work here and be on my way?" Doc said.

Ramsey and Treasure left allowing Doc to complete his examination.

The coffee was hot, the salt pork fried when Doc ambled out into the kitchen. "They're both doing better than I expected," he stated. "I told Cora she could venture out of bed to sit in the rockin' chair for a few hours over the next couple days. After that, she can resume moderate daily chores, but no heavy lifting for a month."

"Understood, Doc. I'll make sure she abides by your instructions," Ramsey assured.

Doc squeezed Treasure's shoulder. "Boy, you reckon them hens of yours got an egg or two this mornin'? Sure would go good with that bacon you're pa's fried up, and I've hungered up an appetite, it seems." Treasure waited for a nod of approval from his father. "Walk, don't run, son. You might find yourself a bit dizzy until you get your legs under you."

"I'll mosey out there and back, Papa." Treasure, like a toy with a broken wheel, made his way to the door and out to the porch.

"I wanted the boy out of ear-shot, Ramsey," Doc said.

"There's not something wrong, is there?"

"Oh, no. I only wanted to let you know that you and Cora can resume your lovemaking in another couple weeks' time. Her bleeding has nearly stopped, but I want to make sure there's no bed activity for a while yet, so as not to start it up again. She's lost too much as it is." Doc took it upon himself to pour a cup of coffee, then sat at the table. "She most likely won't have her woman time until she stops nursing. Most women don't, but want to be sure there's no tangling the bed sheets for another ten days or so."

"I'll be sure to remember, Doc." Hell, Ramsey didn't know if he and Cora would ever get to the place where making love was something they'd share—willingly, consciously.

When the meal preparation was complete, Ramsey took a plate to Cora along with a cup of weakened coffee. He kissed both his wife and daughter on the forehead. "I'll be back to check on you as soon as Doc leaves."

"If I'm sleeping, please wake me, Ramsey. I enjoy your visits." Cora took his hand in hers and nuzzled it against her cheek.

"You can count on it, wife."

When he sat down with Doc and Treasure to eat breakfast, there was one thing Ramey knew for sure. One morning, real soon, he'd sit at this table with Cora, and he'd reach across and take her hands in his. He'd tell her he loved her, only her. He figured that was something she ought to know.

As fate would have it, that morning in the future never came. Later that night when he'd got Treasure tucked into bed, he went in to say goodnight to Cora and Odetta. He eased himself down on the bed so as not to wake the sleeping baby.

"Why were you willing to give this child your name, Ramsey?" Cora asked.

"Why do you think, Cora?"

"Were you trying to save her the gossip of the town biddies, like when you married me?"

Ramsey tenderly brushed his hand against Cora's cheek. "When I agreed to our marriage that was a big part of the reason, to spare you and my son any ill talk. But things have changed since then."

206

"Changed? How?" Cora asked.

"Cora, all the months you carried the baby, I grew to love her...think of her as my own. I didn't know if you'd permit me to give her my name, claim her as my child, but I hoped you would. In my heart, she is my baby, even though I didn't plant the seed. Can you understand that?"

"I can because that's how I feel about Treasure." Cora lowered her eyes and sighed, then returned her gaze to Ramsey. "There's one thing."

"And what would that be, Mrs. Locke?"

When Odetta is old enough to understand, I do want her to know about William...the man I was married to when I got pregnant." She sighed again. "He was a good man, and if he'd lived, he would have been a loving father. I hope you can understand the need to tell her, Ramsey."

"Sweet Cora. I wouldn't want it another way. If it weren't for him, I'd not have Odetta in my life to cherish the way I do. I owe him, don't you figure?"

"Thank you, Ramsey." She stroked his arm affectionately. "It's more than I could have hoped for, it gives me great joy to know you want Odetta to carry the Locke name...be a part of...."

"Our family, Cora? We have become a family, a real honest-to-goodness family." Ramsey affirmed.

"I'm still the woman you agreed to marry out of concern for her reputation."

"I did." Ramsey leaned down and gave her a tender but passionate kiss. "But, I'd marry you again this minute, because I've fallen deeply in love with you."

"You have? You love me?"

"Only you, Cora Blythe Locke, now and forever."

Cora circled her free arm around Ramsey's waist and rested her hand against his shoulder, stroking affectionately. "I've loved you for so long, Ramsey. I wanted to tell you, but I didn't think you felt the same. I thought you were still in love with Caroline."

"I loved Caroline just as you loved William. Our past will always hold fond memories of them, Cora, but it doesn't define our future. My future is with you and our children."

"Oh, Ramsey, I am so overjoyed. My love for you fills me."

"Well, woman, you tend to getting healed, and soon we can show each other the bounty of love there is between us."

"Ummm, I can't wait."

"Yeah, I'll be marking the days off the calendar and making arrangements for Treasure to stay over with Henry Hollister," Ramsey vowed.

They both laughed and embraced one another.

Cora's heart threatened to burst with the love she felt for Ramsey, for her son and baby daughter. At long last, she had the family she'd always dreamed of having. Her long journey filled with unexpected obstacles had brought her here, to the Lost C Ranch. It brought her home. She was content. She was loved. She was blessed.

Epilogue

Winter had come and gone. The seeds were in the ground for corn. The potato eyes were in the cellar awaiting end of the year planting. Treasure led old Sara around in the yard. "Jus' 'cuz I can't get on your back no more, girl, don't mean I don't love ya. I do."

Cora hung clothes on the line and grinned, listening to Treasure assure the mule.

"I've noticed Sara isn't nearly as sure-footed with the loss of one eye. No sense in taxing her, if we don't have a need. She's had enough hard times. We'll want to give her plenty of rest so she'll be able to pull the plow come planting time," Ramsey explained.

"I reckon tillin' the field is enough of a job for an old mule like Sara," Treasure agreed.

"I'm proud of your compassion and understanding, son. I know she thanks you for caring, even though she can no longer carry you on her back."

Sara's work reprieve however, did include daily walks in the yard, like today Treasure leading her so she didn't run into anything.

After lunch Ramsey steered the wagon around to the front of the house. "Cora, I'm going to town and do a bit of trading." He sat on the wagon seat, tied to the rear were two young beef cows. "I'll be back for supper," he said and pulled away.

The sun was three fingers above the horizon when Ramsey returned, a Palomino pony in tow. He saw Cora watching from the kitchen window as he pulled the wagon into the barn. Once he'd unhooked the team, he came into the house.

"What have you done, Ramsey Locke?"

He grinned at Cora. "Reckoned the boy needed a little something to fill the void since Sara's not a riding mule anymore." Ramsey knew his son would have to mount the pony from the porch for some time to come, but one day he'd grow enough to stirrup into the saddle.

"Treasure," Ramsey called.

"Yes, Papa?" Treasure strolled from his room, looking like a wet puppy.

"I got you something while I was in town today."

"Is it one of them striped candy sticks I like?" His face lit up.

"Better than that. Why don't you run out to the barn and see? Check the wagon."

You could hear the child's excitement from the kitchen. "I'd better go see if he's still walking on the ground," Ramsey said.

Cora picked up Odetta. "We'll go with you."

They found Treasure stroking the horse's neck and rubbing his hand against her nose.

"Want do you think, son? Will she do ya?"

"She's the finest golden pony I ever did see. Is she mine, Papa? All mine?"

"That she is. You'll have to grow into her, but she'll wait for you."

"What will you name her, Treasure?" Cora asked.

He thought for a minute. "Sara's a good old mule, and she'll always be my favorite, but I reckon she wouldn't want me not to hone my ridin' skills. I'm guessin' she'd want me all the way happy." Treasure stroked the pony's neck. "I figure ridin' on the back of this golden horse could do the job. I'm gonna name her Happy."

"That's a mighty fine name, son."

"Thinkin' I oughta ride to the top of Washoo Ridge, Papa. Take a look-see at the cattle grazin' on the other side."

"All right, but don't go where I can't see you from the yard," Ramsey instructed and pulled a small tan leather saddle from the wagon. He secured the cinch and placed the bridle reins on the pommel.

Treasure hopped up on the wagon bed and straddled the pony. She whinnied and nodded her head. "Come on, Sara," he called when he saw the mule in the yard. "You can come with us, girl." Treasure sat tall, held the bridle rein in both hands and rode up the hill, the mule trailing close behind.

Ramsey observed Treasure and the horse from the porch steps where he sat. The sky was blue and the breeze gentle. Detty, as they all called her now, sat on a blanket in a wooden box playing with a rattle he'd fashioned from a piece of poplar and dried corn kernels.

Cora gathered eggs from the hen house. He watched his pregnant wife stretch and place a hand on her back. She was only a few months along, but already heavy with child. He'd vowed not to stray far from home until she gave birth, determined to be with her this time from beginning to end.

"I love you," Cora yelled and blew him a kiss.

He reached up, grabbed it from the air and stuck it into his shirt pocket "I'll save this for when I'm alone up in the north acreage riding herd."

She smiled and stooped again to search for eggs.

Ramsey picked up Detty and placed her on his lap, taking her tiny hands in his, playing patty-cake. "Little girl, your papa is a mighty content man."

The child pulled a hand free and pushed her fingers against Ramsey's lips, "Pa...pa."

The smile that widened Ramsey's face, hearing the baby's first words, could light up the night sky like an Aurora Borealis. Yes, he was about as happy as a man had a right to be.

Cora saw Ramsey lift Odetta onto his lap, kiss her fingers and laugh at her jabber. He was a perfect father, and Detty had captured his heart. She was overjoyed that she and Ramsey were having a child of their own. It would be a winter birth, but this time Ramsey vowed he'd be with her when the baby came. Together they would welcome this new addition to their family. Treasure hoped for a little brother, but she knew he'd love another sister all the same. He was the best big brother anyone could hope to have. He doted on Detty and entertained her while she and Ramsey were busy with chores.

She gazed up the hill and waved to her son. The new pony seemed to know she had a precious bundle on her back. The mare took small, careful steps along the ridge top.

Cora never imagined such a life would unfold when she'd arrived in Rabbit Glen, Texas, nearly two years ago. Ramsey had changed the sign on the fence at the entrance to the yard. Now it read RC Ranch. A tribute to the love she and Ramsey shared.

The wind blew a gentle warm breeze. It caressed Cora and cooled her damp skin. Her heart expanded with the love that filled it. Life was good. There was nothing she longed for that didn't already exist in her world. Yes, she was about as happy as a woman had a right to be.

The End

Author Bio

Sunny Marie Baker has written stories ever since she could hold a pencil in her hand and form letters into words. As an only child, living in rural Missouri, she had many imaginary playmates, and those friends became characters in the childhood stories she wrote.

As an adult, in between parenting and working in the business end of the medical field, she published eleven short stories, some written with a co-author. Cora's Promise is her debut novel.

Sunny Marie Baker lives in a beautiful mountain area near Yosemite National Park in central California. She shares a home with her husband, Bob and their two dogs, Fannee and Hessee.

Cora's Promise is book one in the Texas Strong Series, to be followed by Claree's Plan and Camille's Purpose.

Check out the author's web site: sunnymariebaker.com, or you can send her a note at: sunnymariebaker@gmail.com

Made in the USA
Middletown, DE
18 October 2022